[Type here]

MW00413969

In Dangers Eyes

(My Brother's Keeper)

ISBN-13: 978-1500773007

ISBN-10: 150077300X

Library of Congress Control Number: 2014939903

First Print March 2016

Printed in the United States

Dedicated to the Fallen Soldiers of the 1980's and 1990's crack epidemic…

Nine-year-old Danny loved spending time with his grandfather. He would sit around for hours listening to his Grandpa's stories. Danny had an entire weekend with his grandfather and he knew he would enjoy every minute of it. While grandpa was in the kitchen making tea, Danny picked up an old dusty photo album. Danny was stuck on the first photo, it was a picture, there were five men sitting around a 600 Mercedes Benz. One man stood out, he had on a waist length mink, two gold chains, all his fingers were covered with gold and diamonds, and he had two 45 automatics tucked in his waistline. Grandpa walked in,

"Dammit boy, you always touchin somethin", he said with a smile on his face.

"Who's these men Grandpa?"

"Whew", Grandpa said looking at the picture, he sat down and smiled,

"These men here, hmm hum, these used to be the baddest men in Harlem, sit down, let me tell you a story."

Right away Grandpa had little Danny's full attention.

"You see this man here", Grandpa said pointing to the man in the mink,

"That there, is Daniel 'Danger' Warren."

"Daniel, grandpa just like my name?"

"Yeah, you're actually named after him, now be quiet and let me tell the story."

Daniel Warren was born about `69 in Harlem Hospital. From the day he was born, some said he was doomed. His father Martin 'Showtime' Warren had become one of the biggest dope dealers in the game, after his boss Nelson Brooks went to prison. Imagine your father being the biggest dope dealer in the city and your mother being one of the biggest addicts. Vivian Warren was a Glamour Girl in the seventies, which were controlled by Martin. Vivian was known as the Hoods "Diahann Carroll". As Martin's money grew, so did Vivian's habit. She was truly a victim of Martin's product, which he had no choice but to feed her.

Daniel had everything a child could possibly want. His father had the `73 Oldsmobile 98, Danny had the same exact model kiddie car, not like the power wheels you kids have today, back then you had to pedal. I remember back when they were threatening James Johnson, yeah the white folks been wanting Harlem as long as anyone could remember. They wanted to close the Apollo due to violation an old crooked inspector found. James couldn't find anyone to invest in the old theater; the white banks couldn't give two shits about the place, nor the apes that loved the jungle music. With time running out and nowhere else to go, James Johnson went to Martin in tears.

Now Martin was all about Black power, he would donate to everything Black. It was once said he gave NOI a few thousand, even tossed the NAACP some money, but who'd admit to taking money from a dope dealer.

Martin knew how much the Apollo meant to Harlem; shit with all the history there, it was Harlem. Martin gave Johnson, who was a complete stranger at the time, 300 gees to get the place up and running again. After that, they began calling Martin 'Showtime'. The eighties started off fucked up, as the streets were making the transition from Heroin to crack, so was Daniel's mother. Ronald Reagan, an actor, had taken control of the country and his wife had started her bullshit just say "NO" campaign. Crack was fucking up the game, you see with dope you had to have money to make the money, but under Reagan, cocaine dropped to almost 12 dollars a gram. Everyone and their mommas was dealing, the game changed drastically.

Showtime was an entirely different breed, if you were around him you had to have money. His workers drove caddies, back then you could get a Caddy for seven gees. Showtime shared everything with his right hand man Ray Roberts AKA Bobby Rich. Showtime loved Bobby like a brother; he always promised Bobby no matter what, he would be straight. For nothing Bobby was his full partner. No doubt about it, Showtime was rich, he had an apartment on 116th street. The master bedroom was filled with money, not one piece of furniture, just money. At one point, there was 13 million, after a while, Showtime lost count.

"This room here Bobby is Danny's, if anything ever happens to me, you make sure Danny gets every cent, you hear me Blood?"

"Of course, he's my God son, if anything ever happened to you, I'd raise him like he was my own."

"Thanks blood, you're my brother. Vivian's lost to that shit. Danny will never be able to rely on her, she gone man, I can't even help her no more", Martin said with tears in his eyes.

In those days, it was almost impossible to get money without having Police on the payroll. Shit they controlled the product, the Italians and the Irish didn't get along, but they both used the blacks to do their dirty work. Since the early seventies, Showtime had been paying off an Irish Detective O'Mayer. O'Mayer had been considered the best cop in the city, what they didn't know was he was one of the biggest dope dealing murders in the game. When Martin first started paying off O'Mayer, he asked for 25 gees a month, which was like having a quarter million in 1976, by '78 it was fifty gees. The 6th of every month, O'Mayer and Showtime would meet on the roof of an apartment building in Kings Towers, which was called Foster Project.

"You know Martin; a lot of these young boys are getting big on this crack shit."

"yeah they are, but that shit is fucking up the game O'Mayer and you know it."

O'Mayer smiled as they both walked to the edge of the roof and stared down at Harlem.

"Look at this shit Martin, half these nigg… motherfuckers, can't read, can't write but all you see in the projects are Cadillac's, Buick's and Oldsmobile's, somethings wrong."

"What you talkin bout Phil?"

"Where'd you go for vacation last year?" O'Mayer asked

Martin smiled as he reminisced,

"Paris." He answered

"You see, that's what I'm talking about. I want to travel. I want to go places I can't pronounce." O'Mayer paused for a moment,

"I want to drive 10 thousand dollar cars." He added

"Phil, you get 600 gees tax free a year, you can afford anything you want."

Quickly the smile on O'Mayer face was gone,

"Martin, I need more."

Martin knew it was coming sooner or later and truthfully Martin himself had grown tired. Crack was ruining the game, in a short time, Martin had watch it take so heartless strongest, most reliable men and turned them in monsters.

"So what does that mean?"

"I want a hundred fifty gees a month."

Martin couldn't help but to laugh,

"Get the fuck outta here Mayer's, are you using this shit? That's 1.8 a year, are you crazy?"

There wasn't the slightest smirk on O'Mayer's face, but he was dead serious.

"You guys do what, a hundred…. hundred fifty gees a day; They think it's fair."

Now Martin understood,

"They, Who…. Carlos?" He asked

"Yeah he's a little unhappy, with this crack thing."

Carlos was the man behind everything. Martin shook his head; he saw it coming but it still shocked him to hear it.

"Man, tell him to take that up with his man Reagan, or maybe, it's time to retire and let these young boys have this shit."

Martin genuinely felt bad, he had grown rich with these men although he had been their untouchable mule.

"tire Martin too what"

O'M r's yelled as if he were on the verge of tears, he hated t. oment he hated what he was supposed to do.

But now M was pissed,

"What! Mother fucker you got pension to fall back on, what the fuck do I have when I die? I'm just dead on this mother fucker"

"What? Martin, if it wasn't for me, you wouldn't have shit. It's been two years since a worker of yours got pinched."

Martin was pissed, but remained calm.

"That's robbery, bottom line."

"Robbery", O'Mayer said now screaming.

"Robbery is what Brooks was doing to you and your little team of hoodlums. Don't you remember those days? when you were, broke and hungry? I made you what you are today," O'Mayer said with spit flying out his mouth.

"And now I'm done, the game is changing. Find one of these young boys, there's a hundred of them down there", Martin said gesturing to the streets below.

"Look at this", O'Mayer said walking to the other side of the roof.

Martin followed he was never once in fear for his life, he and O'Mayer's had grown up in these streets together.

"Look down there; when I first met you, you were selling dime pieces for The B.N.B, without a cent for yourself. Couldn't even buy a soda pop; now…. now look at what you have! Everything you could possibly want, a Black man living the American dream, money, cars, women."

"And now, I quit, I got a son to raise"

O'Mayer couldn't believe what he was hearing, it wasn't that he couldn't find another HNIC, the next one was right there, every 10 out of 50 of them willing to murder for the opportunity, but O'Mayer knew he would never find a man as trustworthy as Martin, definitely not Bobby Rich.

"You quit, you think it's that easy, you can't just walk away".

Martin sucked his teeth,

"I'm through O'Mayer", he turned around, O'Mayer quickly grabbed his Billy club.

"Don't turn your back on me motherfucker" O'Mayer swung,

The blow crashing into the back of Martin's head; he dropped down to one knee, grabbing his head. Winching in pain,

"Fuck, I'll kill you", Martin groaned.

O'Mayer was moving fast, he lifted the club to strike again, Martin pulled out his police issued thirty-eight, the Saturday night special given to him by O'Mayer's himself.

"Is that my gun?", O'Mayer asked

"Put the fucking gun down", O'Mayer yelled.

With one hand holding his head, Martin aimed the gun.

"Motherfucker, put the club down."

O'Mayer laughed,

"What are you gonna do, kill a cop, you, stupid motherfucker." O'Mayer took a few steps towards Martin.

"I ain't playin O'Mayer, the badge ain't fuckin bullet proof."

"You ain't gonna shoot me. I know you better than that."

"Dammit O'Mayer, put the fuckin club down, you had everything, every fuckin thing, now put the club down or…"

"Or what Martin, I'll crack your head wide open", O'Mayer said rushing Martin;

he had no choice (Bang, Bang, Bang). All three shots hit O'Mayer in the chest.

"You…You shot…you shot me." O'Mayer struggled gasping for air.

What the fuck had Martin done, he stood over O'Mayer's dying body. A million things ran through his mind, one thing for sure, Martin had to get out of there. He quickly ran down the roof stairs to the elevator, he began to wipe his own blood off of his face; O'Mayer had been like a brother, believe it or not, they had literally grown up together. Martin was a 19-year-old runner for Nelson Brooks and O'Mayer was a 23-year-old foot Patrol Cop when they had started their business, he just continued to think to himself, what had he done.

O'Mayer's partner, Joe Donahue, was sitting in the parking lot along with Ray Roberts aka Bobby Rich. By the time Martin made it to the ground floor, his blood began to mix with his nervous sweat, he looked like a mad man as he rushed to the car.

"Hey..........Martin...Warren, get over here", Donahue called out, he began to run over to the car. "What the fuck?", Bobby asked.

"Man, just.........just get the fuck outta here", Martin said, still holding his head.

"Stop this fucking car Roberts", Donahue said, grabbing on, as if his one hand could stop the 2-ton car.

"Stop this fucking car", he screamed again, Bobby hit the gas pedal, the tires began to spin, forcing Donahue to let go. The tires screeched as Bobby peeled out of the lot.

Donahue ran into the building. Donahue knew he wasted a valuable three minutes waiting on the elevator, he finally reached the roof.

"Oh God, Phil", he called out, running to his partners' side, grabbing his Walkie talkie

"Officer down, Officer down on the roof of King Towers, Tower 5. Officer needs assistance, immediately."

O'Mayer still gasps for air.

"What?", Donahue asked as O'Mayer tried to say something.

"Ra...Ra...set me."

"Ra set you up?" O'Mayer nodded.

"What's Ra?" Donahue asked.

"Ba, Ba...Ba. B".

It didn't matter how long help took now, O'Mayer was gone. Within an hour, police were everywhere with pictures of Martin there was an all-out man hunt for Martin and they were looking for a cop killer so NYPD were out for full force vengeance...

Martin knew better than to go home, so he went to his girls, Josephine's. Once Vivian had completely given her life to the dope, Martin knew he had to find a woman he could trust and that was Jo. Martin barked orders to close this, go get that, tell so and so this, he knew he had to get out of the state, and then out of the country.

"I gotta get to Newark"

"Airport", Jo asked.

"Yeah, Cuba, maybe Belize, either one I'll be safe."

"I'm goin with you Martin".

He didn't answer but Josephine began packing her things.

"Bobby, everything is on you."

"Dammit, Show don't worry; let's just get you to the airport."

"No, they'll be looking for the both of us", he paused for a moment.

"Jo"

"Yes, Baby"

"Get me a razor, one of your wigs, and a dress."

By the time he and Jo were ready, Martin was completely from head to toe a woman, fake breast and all.

"Bobby, you gotta take care of Daniel…. till I send for him. There's over 25 million in the stash house, take the key. Watch my boy Bobby",

Martin said with tears in his eyes. He hated leaving Daniel more than anything, fuck the money or the cars, even the women. He loved Daniel.

"Hold it down Bobby, the world is yours."

The FBI was all over the 32nd precinct, Donahue had been questioned by everyone. The big question, what was O'Mayer doing on the roof of Kings Towers? And where was Donahue at the time of the shooting. The best thing Donahue could come up with was O'Mayer was meeting with his informant and for everyone's safety he went up by himself.

"Donahue call on line three", Officer Dunleavy called into

the room.

"This is Donahue."

"Donahue." Donahue knew who it was right away.

"What the fuck do you want? You're a dead man, do you know that" Donahue whispered

"I didn't know what was goin on."

"Yeah, right."

"Listen, Martin's headed to Newark Airport right now in a gold Cadillac Eldorado, license plate NY41969. They'll be two women in the car, one is Martin. He's got about twenty minutes on you."

(Click) The line went dead. Donahue had all the info he needed, within the next 35 minutes Martin was in custody. Donahue had phoned in the car and its occupants descriptions. He gave direct orders to New Jersey State Troopers to pull the car over and detain it, no arrest or searches were to be done until he arrived.

Donahue performed the search finding 23 million dollars and 10 kilos of pure heroin. The case was turned over to the feds due to the murder of police officer Phillip O'Mayer. Martin 'Showtime' Warren was sentenced to 165 years to life in prison. In New York, a black man could be anything a doctor, a lawyer, a killer, anything, but not a cop killer. Josephine James was sentenced to 50 months in Federal Prison for aiding and abetting a fugitive.

## THE BEGINNING:

Showtime was gone and forgotten, Vivian's habit was ten times worse; she was now doing everything to get high. Even bobby was taking advantage of her addiction, Bobby also did nothing he promised, by then Daniel was raising himself. Bouncing from family member to member, but once they realized there was no money coming, Daniel had to go. The year Daniel turned 12 in 1982, Vivian was known as one of Bobby's whores, they were partying this particular night, Bobby and Vivian had been arguing over dope. It was said Vivian had embarrassed him badly since he wouldn't give her any dope. She left to go turn a trick, two days later they found her body in an alleyway with her throat slit. Rumor had it; one of her Johns tried to get over for a ten-dollar blow job. She began to fight him and he cut her throat.

Now Daniel really had no one, he would sleep in abandoned cars and rundown buildings. To eat, he would get up early and wait for the bread trucks to make their drop offs and he'd steal rolls and bagels, only enough to feed his hunger. For a few dollars he'd sweep the local barber shops. That was how he kept his feet fresh. He was dirty from the ankles up, but sneakers he kept up to speed. When he was fourteen, he was cleaning the game room for Old Man Jenkins. He liked Old Man Jenkins and the Old Man liked him, but this day as Daniel swept and washed the windows, a local kid about sixteen decided to make fun of Daniels misfortune. Daniel ignored him, until he called his mother an old crack whore.

Daniel blacked out, he beat the kid blind in one eye, 3 years in Juvenile detention, his first bid but far from his last. That's where he met Lance Palmer, also known as L.P., a fourteen-year-old murderer from Brooklyn. Lance had beaten his stepfather to death with an aluminum baseball bat. He was tired of the mental and physical abuse against him and his mother. Of course, during the trial his mother testified against him. Both young men easily formed a kinship with each other. Neither one of them had anyone else in life to care for them, so they held each other down; they started saying they were cousins. Daniel was 17, a year later Lance would be released.

With nowhere to go, Daniel was released to a shelter in Bellevue Medical Center. It was fucked up in the shelter, but it was a place to sleep. It was 1988; minimum wage was only 3.25 an hour. Daniel got a job working as a messenger in mid-town. It was hell walking around Manhattan in the winter, but with his first paycheck, he was able to buy some clothes. He spent a hundred on three shirts, but he still wore the tight buddy lees from DFY. Daniel tried his best not to think about the past, he just couldn't wait for L.P. to get home from DFY. That night Daniel laid in his cot, just staring at the ceiling, as hard as he tried, he was unable to ignore thoughts of his mother. Just then a woman began to scream someone was touching her, there was a guard at the door. Daniel stood up to see what was going on. A crack head was harassing a woman, everyone ignored her screams, and then Daniel saw she had a daughter. He couldn't watch any longer. He ran over to help. The crack fiend jumped up.

"Nigga is you crazy", he screamed.

Daniel caught him with a left hook. The woman grabbed her daughter as Daniel pummeled the fiend; finally, the guard ran over and grabbed Daniel. He was put out of the shelter, there was no fighting allowed. Daniel couldn't help but think, no fighting, but rape was okay. Daniel walked the streets for hours, it was freezing. Daniel found an auto body shop with old cars parked around it. There was an old van, the door was open, and so he crawled into it. He was still cold, but it was warmer than outside.

"Hey, kid get the fuck outta there."

Daniel jumped up; he grabbed his bag and ran. It was after 10 am, so he was late for work. He jumped on the train. His boss was a short fat balding man named Nick; he was an asshole, a real racist bastard. When Daniel walked in,

"Hey", Nick said.

"You know boy, the only thing worse than an old nigger is a young nigger."

Before Nick knew it, he was sitting on his back pockets holding his eye.

"Get out, get out you little piece of shit before I call the police."

That was the last thing Daniel needed, for the first time in years he went uptown to King Towers or Foster Projects. He walked around; everything at least looked the same. Now he was dead broke with nowhere to sleep. But even early in the morning dudes were on every corner and dudes were getting money.

It was a lot different from when his father was around, there were only a few hustlers, now it seemed like every corner had hustlers or 5 percenters. Daniel didn't have many friends growing up because of his father's paranoia, but a lot of people recognized him. He would hear people mumble and whisper as he walked by. 145th and Convent, to walk up that block, which might have been the worst mistake Daniel had ever made.

"Young Blood", the voice called.

Daniel looked around.

"Danny warren, dammit boy you look just like Yo momma, boy what you doin round these parts?"

"Just walkin round sir."

"Sir, boy you don't know who I am", the man asked.

Daniel just shook his head no.

"Boy, I'm Ray Roberts." Daniel still shook his head.

"Bobby Rich."

"Oh, you use to be with my dad."

"Yeah, me and your dad was partners. I was actually with him the day he got picked up by the feds, shit Harlem died that day. Boy where you headed?"

"Nowhere, I got nowhere to go."

"C'mon in, I'll get you something to eat."

They went inside the store front number spot; Bobby ordered some fish and French fries. They sat around and talked about the past, Martin, and Vivian's death, they talked about life with Danny's family members and D.F.Y. When they got to the present, Bobby was upset.

"What you mean you was workin for the white man? Let me tell you something young blood, there's three things in America that aren't meant for a black man, school, work and the constitution. Don't you ever let me hear you workin for no white man."

"So, Mr. Rich, what can I do? I have no money, no place to sleep."

"Don't worry, you like family, I got you."

The words sent a chill down Daniels back, he heard those words so many times before, your family, your like family, and everyone who said those words to him had ulterior motives. He prayed silently that Bobby Rich didn't. That night Bobby took him to an old run down Brownstone on 126th.

"You can camp out here for a while, it's a little fucked up, but it's warm at night. Don't worry Danny, in a few months you'll be on top of the world. You just have to prove your loyalty son." They walked to the ground floor apartment of the Brownstone. Bobby knocked on the door, a small hole just big enough to fit a fist through opened, the person behind the door looked at both of them, and then opened up. It was a woman, hard to explain, she wasn't pretty but she also wasn't ugly. Maybe she had been pretty at one time but as of right then she was just Mookie, the crack head whom Danny would be living with for the next few months. They were Inside the biggest crack spot in Harlem, Danny would quickly learn the game and wouldn't complain the winter was cold, so he just gave thanks.

## William Bradshaw

William Bradshaw grew up in the polo grounds, the youngest of three children. His parents taught him the benefits of hard work and he followed their lead. He was determined to make it out of the projects and with the help of his brother Philip, who was the oldest followed by his sister Monica. Philip was the main one to keep his foot in Williams ass, when it seemed like he was slacking, William straightened right up. When you say hard work, Willy was the epitome of the word when his college class mates put in 40 hours working, Willy put in 50 never taking a break and graduating fourth in his class, he felt it was because of his color. Now here he was, he could have been any kind of lawyer, but due to his dilemma with his graduating class he chose criminal law. Like many others, he wanted to make a difference, as if he could.

"Counselor", Judge Angic called.

It was closing arguments for young Mario Lindsay and it hadn't gone good. Twenty-four-year-old Mario had taken the NYPD detectives on a high speed chase, from Washington Heights to Broadway by Yonkers, causing two Westchester police cruisers to crash. The officers were in critical condition at the time, but were now stable enough to testify. His Explorer had careened into a lamp post and the police officers hit his SUV with a barrage of gunfire, over 27 shots. Willy Bradshaw stood up and took a deep breath, he cleared throat,

"Ahem".

He had been in this situation many times before, but of course there was more, 2 kilos of cocaine and a glock nineteen with the serial numbers scratched off.

"Ladies and Gentlemen......., you've heard testimonies from New York's finest, as well as Yonkers P.D and many times they have been justified, but we know plenty of times our NYPD has used excessive force, uncalled for measures. We can go back as far as Eleanor Bumper, a harmless old woman. Now, don't get me wrong, I am in no way comparing Mister Lindsay to a 70-year-old woman, by no means."

William now removed his glasses and rubbed his eyes with his thumb and index fingers of his left hand.

"Twenty-seven shots", he said shaking his head as if the thought alone saddened him.

"The man had hit a light post for goodness sake, the car was stopped, but I can't let you forget the terrified flight my client took. Have any of you noticed not one officer during testimony mentioned identifying themselves as the police?"

This drew a reaction from everyone in the audience, including the jurors, there was a low murmur throughout the courtroom forcing Judge Angic to bang his gavel and call for order. "Yes, your honor, that is what we need, order and justice. I need each and every one of you to close your eyes, imagine walking out your front door."

He paused as he gave everyone a moment.

"Now as you leave your home, you look up the street and see a man running full speed, all due respect to Cuomo and Koch, but our streets aren't the safest so you rush to your car, you get in, before you notice there's some man yielding a gun, banging on your window, no badge, just a big silver gun. Do you open the window and ask does he need help or do you get the hell out of there?" He paused again.

"Do any of you remember David Berkowitz, the Son of Sam? This case isn't about what Mario does for a living may I remind you, the officers had no idea what they were gonna find. This wasn't an ongoing investigation, this was a mistaken identity and out of fear, my client ran. Not one blue and white, not one siren, all unmarked cars. Mario was scared for his life, he made a decision anyone of us would have made. No, let me not say that. Now let me say this, the officers involved made the decision not to identify themselves, nothing further."

William Bradshaw had given several closing arguments, this may have been his worst one, but this was a case he knew he couldn't win. Out of twenty trials he had only lost two, he knew this would be his third. It took no time for the jury to find a verdict. In ten minutes the foreman read a verdict of not guilty. Bradshaw had done it again.

Reggie Stagalini, known as Stags had worked for the Carposi crime family for years. The boss known as Jimmy 'The Snake' Carposi had sent Stags down to keep an eye on

William and see how good the kid really was. Stag's nudged Teets,

"Hey the fuckin Moolie pulled it off."

"Yeah, the kids good", Teets replied.

"You think he's what's the boss is looking for", Teets now asked.

"We'll see."

Carposi Family:

Jimmy Carposi had once controlled the heroin trade in uptown New York, but that was all changing. Dope was one thing, but it was as if an invisible force called NAFTA in control of cocaine and Carposi wanted in Harper Bakemen the United States Attorney for the Southern District of New York was the door to the cocaine trade. Bakemen had many positions available in his organization, but Cuomo and Koch wouldn't play ball, so the judicial section which was Bakemen's field looked shaky in New York. The president had literally flooded the country with cocaine through NAFTA. Bakemen Just needed a good lawyer that could be bought, to take his position someone he could make District Attorney, which would play his kind of game, and by giving New York City its first black DA , Bakemen would be mayor or governor in a few years. That's when Bakemen found a young black man named William Bradshaw, but William wouldn't play ball. So

Bakemen put the Vice on Carposi, who then squeezed Bradshaw.

"Willy my man", Reggie called out,

"Congratulations on another one." Reggie extended his hand;

Willy ignored it and continued to pack his briefcase.

"Come on Willy don't be so rude, I thought you niggers were humble since doctor king got it", Teets added.

Willy fought hard to keep his composure.

"Willy, please, the boss wants to talk wit ya."

"I'm not interested. Tell your boss, tell Bakemen and any other corrupted fuckers that this nigger's not for sale."

William finished packing his briefcase, slammed it shut and walked away. He had to admit it felt good standing for something and his race, but he knew he was dealing with dangerous men.

That night he planned on having dinner with his lovely wife Sandra and her parents. Now they were uppity Mulatto, until he had brought the house in Westchester, they had never given him any credit. To them he was just a lucky nappy headed nigger out of the projects. At times Sandra was just like them. They were having dinner at Ché LaFrance in the dining section of Manhattan, a real classy place, overpriced meals for never enough portions. William got dress in his office, a nice smoke gray Isaac

Mizrahi three piece, no tie necessary. As he approached the table, Sandra was the only one to stand. She hugged him.

"Baby, I heard you've won another big one", Sandra said boastfully for her husband.

"Please dear, do not gloat for a freed murder or worse", replied her father, Mr. Jefferson.

"Please Charles, even the poor and unfortunate need representation."

"Please Ellen; the men he represents are low life scum, men that sell guns and drugs to children."

"Please father", Sandra, Said interrupting.

William still hadn't sat down, just then,

"Mr. William Bradshaw"; the man said extending his hand.

"Attorney General Bakemen."

"Attorney General, it's an honor", Mr. Jefferson said standing and extending his hand.

"Oh please, ah."

"Mr. Charles Jefferson."

"Please sir have a seat, this man here is the one you should be honored to be with. I've been trying to have dinner with him for months, William why haven't you returned any of my calls." William sat down, resting his forehead in the palm of his hands.

"Because Bakemen I am not interested."

"Excuse him Attorney General Bakemen."

"No don't excuse me. Bakemen excuse us, we're trying to have dinner."

"Yes, but please give me a call. I really could use a lawyer of your caliber in my office." "Never", William added as Bakemen and his goons walked away.

"Boy are you mad, I am convinced Ellen, this boy is on drugs."

"Father, please."

"No Sandra, your husband is so obsessed with the hood he's a flipping idiot."

William slammed his hand on the table startling the restaurants patrons, also knocking over glasses. He then jumped up and walked out the door. He'd been fed up with her parents for years and this was it. He wouldn't go home that night; he'd sleep at his office.

Bakemen sat in the back seat of the Lincoln Continental.

"This nigger wants to play hardball; I want every piece of dirt you can get on him. I want to know every woman he's ever dealt with. Shit, I want every man his mother's slept with", he was quiet for a moment.

"Carlos will work on him; also maybe a little pressure can get a few things done."

Harper Bakemen literally earned the position he was in now, in the middle of his second term and both elections he used intimidation to eliminate his opposing candidates. His first election there was a Democrat Alan Crocher whose 19-year-old daughter overdosed on pure heroin. Samantha Crocher had never touched a beer much less a drug in her 19 years. She was found in her 1977 Volvo coupe with the needle still in her arm.

This past election, Jeremy Caan, a Republican was sure to win. He'd been in the lead for almost 4 months. New York was ready for a change and 1983 promised to be different, with stricter drug and gun laws, more federally funded, and after school programs. Attorney General Caan would be the difference New York needed. Until one afternoon Caan's doorbell rang, it was a deliveryman with an envelope. Caan signed for it not expecting anything unusual. Once inside, Caan opened it and dropped the contents on the floor in shock. At once he called his wife. She ran into the living room, he showed her what the delivery man had just dropped off. It was several pictures of their 10-month old baby in the baby's room, someone was holding a gun to the baby's head. Then there was a picture with someone holding a knife at the baby's throat. The back of the picture with knife read,

'So easily it could have ended. Give your child the

opportunity at life; give your family the opportunity. New York is no longer the place for you or your young family. Jeremy trust us, I doubt your infants murder would have been considered a suicide. Ha, Ha, Ha.'

The next day Caan not only dropped out of the race for Attorney General, he also packed up and moved out of New York. Bakemen was right, pressure did get things done. Now the question was how William Bradshaw would react to a little pressure.

SOLDIERS:

Bobby's new soldier was quickly becoming the man, not only was Danny loyal but he took no shit. All Bobby Rich had to do was give the word and the beast was unleashed. His first four months in the game it's said Danny had killed over four men. Now Bobby's problem was his operation was too big for him to control by himself, but he was too selfish and stubborn to get help. His team consisted of Young Danny and the fiends that sold his drugs. Bobby was too worried someone would make more money than him, which had always been his problem. Reggie Stagalini had set up a meeting, Bobby was scared to death. Jimmy Carposi wasn't the type of man that could be reasoned with and Stags his mouthpiece was just as ruthless.

"Bobby fuckin fish", Stag said sarcastically, but his words upset Danny.

"His names Bobby Rich, show fuckin respect."

"Whoa, whoa who's the arrogant Moolie", Stags asked.

"Excuse my nephew", Bobby submissively answered.

"Anyway", Stags replied, looking at the two goons with

him Teets and Moochie.

"Jimmy wants to know your answer on his deal."

"I'm still thinking about it; you know it doesn't seem fair."

"Fair, Bobby, fair. You want fair? This ain't `65 with the Moolie King, what you gotta fuckin dream. Fair is allowing you to still operate. We could shut you and the rest of the nigger nation down", Stags was yelling now.

"What." Danny jumped up.

"What the fuck did you say"

"Ah, calm down."

"Yo, fuck calm down." Danny yelled

Teets and Moochie stood up, quickly Danny pulled out the twin 45's.

"Sit the fuck down."

"Kid, are you fuckin crazy", Teets asked.

"Sit the fuck down everybody." The three Italians obeyed.

"Oh God, Danny what the hell are you doin?"

"Relax Bobby, these disrespectful motherfuckers are through, the fuckin mob don't run shit no more, you fags is finished, especially in Harlem. So tell Jimmy Carposi, Danny Warren said 'Suck a fuckin dick'. Get up Bobby, we're leaving."

With that Bobby and Danny slowly crept out the side door.

"What the fuck have you done", Bobby asked once they were safely in his car.

"What?"

"Do you know who those men were, oh God, you're just like your father." Danny grabbed one of his guns.

"What the fuck does that mean", he asked, pointing the 45 at Bobby.

"Your crazy man, you tryin to get us killed."

"Bobby, the mob is finished. Jamaicans done ran them out the Bronx. Now they just running around like scavengers, tryin to find someone who'll respect their punk asses, fuck them." "Danny, I'm the boss. You can't make decisions for the team without discussing it."

"What team Bobby? Me, Frenchy and Mookie.........matter of fact just, drop me off at Mookie's."

Danny had no fear of the mafia, it was slowly dying. Gotti was coming up fast but he didn't give a fuck about the drug game, but Danny knew what he had to do. It was time to start forming his own team. For the first time he saw the weakness in Bobby Rich. First thing he did was pay a fiend to drive him to upstate New York to see 'L.P." Lance Palm

"It's good to see you, cousin. I thought you forgot about

me."

"Nah, I'm just waitin for you to get home"

"You look good. What you up to."

That's what Danny had been waiting for; he told L.P. everything, even the incident with the mob and how he wanted to start a team. L.P. was proud of his boy and was more anxious to get home than he had ever been.

(Frenchy's Son) Number 1 Draft Pick

Frenchy's story was different, at one time he had been one of the most feared men in Harlem and he had been about money. In the late sixties, he had messed with a woman named Rebecca Morris, who later became Mrs. Reba Nelson Brooks. Brooks had been the second biggest dealer in Harlem, he tried to be like Bumpy Johnson, but years later Brooks would rat on his entire team. Anyway, Adrian Walker was in the same boat as Danny, his mom was also a fiend. Only difference was Vivian was dead and Adrian's mom Alice was the walking dead. She had H.I.V. from intravenous drug use. Adrian was an All-State Running Back in high school. He had over 9 schools offering him full athletic scholarship. He turned down UCLA, Rutgers, Florida, LSU and several other big schools. He wanted to go to a black school, so he chose Morgan State in Alabama.

By this time, L.P. had hooked Danny up with King James, a notorious thug out of Brooklyn. King James crew was known throughout New York as the Decons. King didn't hustle, he robbed motherfuckers and he didn't care who, rappers, singers, actors and now he saw a big investment. Danny knew nothing about sports but they were headed to Fredrick Douglas Academy for a graduation, that was where Danny met Fame Anderson, the 5 foot 2 inch, 140 pound, hazel eyed, brown hair, 19-year-old track star, she was also graduating. But that day it was about Adrian Walker. King James introduced them. Adrian had heard stories of Danny's father growing up, what Danny learned that day was Adrian was on his way to being the man and King was already sticking his hands in the young athlete's pockets.

Adrian's first season at Morgan State, he rushed for over 3,274 yards and 29 touchdowns. By then L.P. was home and he and Danny had Harlem on smash. Once L.P. came home, the robbery game had stepped up and although Danny was a hustler his name somehow always surfaced in a robbery. Decons were feared throughout New York. They were over forty deep in every party. They controlled the scene but still Danny was Bobby's mule. And even L.P. was ready to make a move, but they had no connect.

Game Time

Adrian was the man through his college career but academically he was failing bad, but do to his work on the field they had no choice but to pass him. When he first met Alexis, he fell in love. After their first few months, he brought a 15-thousand-dollar ring. Adrian hung with Decons hard the first football season, over 30 of them took a trip to the Caymans. Adrian didn't give a fuck about anything but football. It was his sophomore year; Coach Johnson called him into his office.

"Adrian, have you looked at your grades this semester?"

"No sir." Coach Johnson just shook his head.

"What are you gonna do if football doesn't work?"

"You buggin right", Adrian said with a little chuckle.

"This is not a joke Adrian. You have to think about life without football."

"Coach there's nothing else. I'm goin pro, that's a fact everybody in the country knows it."

There was nothing anyone could say to Adrian, even Alexis tried to get him to pay more attention to his grades, but even her efforts were useless. His idea when they said work harder was spending more time in the weight room and it paid off 1985 season, he rushed for 3,883 yards, a college record followed by Bo Jackson who ended up winning the Heisman that year. After that season, L.P, King James, Adrian, and Danny all brought matching 1985 BMW 325I Drop Tops. By this time Decons were over 100 strong, mostly in Brooklyn, which had the murder rate for the 80's.

Reggie Stags and Jimmy Carposi sat at their regular table in Stags mother's restaurant. As they were prepared to discuss business with two of the most powerful men in New York City, Attorney General Bakemen and then Police Commissioner Joseph Donahue, the same man that had arrested Showtime almost ten years ago. The meeting was about the crack epidemic in Harlem and the Bronx, not how to stop it, but how to get a bigger piece of it.

"Word on the street is your old friend Ray Roberts is doing over five hundred gees a month", Stags said to the commissioner.

"Oh yeah, we'll he should be easy to fuckin squeeze"

"Yeah, well he's got some asshole nigger workin for em, this kid is a real fuckin prick", Carposi replied.

"What's his name", asked Bakemen. Stags pulled out a sheet of paper,

"Hey, Daniel Warren"

"Daniel Warren", Donahue repeated.

"Why does that name sound so fuckin familiar", he scratched at his head.

"Warren, Warren get the fuck outta here, he's not Martin's kid, is he?" Carposi nodded.

"Listen, Roberts is not a problem, I'll handle him, and he's done business for me in the past. What Harper and I need from you guys….is him, Ernesto Mendoza Arroyo", Donahue said passing the picture across the table.

Arroyo had quickly become one of the biggest cocaine distributors in the Bronx. Bakemen's own people told tales of how good the man's coke was. Even friends of Reagan, himself, praised it potency and this had Bakemen pissed. Neither party took its time on the others mission. Three days after the meeting, Donahue stood on top of the roof his partner had died on years before. "Bobby Rich, you gotta be a millionaire by now."

"Yeah, you too."

"I can't lie, I'm doin pretty good for myself, but you, bein up here has got to send chills through your spine, but then again I hear Warren's son is working for you." Bobby just nodded.

"your A heartless bastard, does he even know?"

"Look Donahue, what the fuck are we doin up here?"

"I gotta offer you can't refuse."

"I'm listening."

"Well, as I said, there's no turnin this down, but I understand you're doing at least 600 a month." Although Bobby shook his head no, Donahue knew it was true.

"Well, I'm offering you full service."

"What are you running, a gas station."

"Ha, that's a good one, but I'll provide protection. I'll let you know when locals, as well as feds, I even have a connect for you."

"Let me guess, Jimmy Carposi."

"Ah, still as sharp as a razor I see."

Bobby began to think about the day O'Mayer died right on this same roof, he thought about killing Donahue right there. But it would be far worse than killing O'Mayer, Donahue was the commissioner.

"Don't get any smart idea Bobby, just say yes."

"So what's the deal?"

"100 gees a month and every now and then you throw me a little fish."

"You couldn't possibly need this money Donahue."

"It's not for me. It's for Carposi, who was ready to offer you a better deal, but you allowed Warren to fuck that up. Just think, soon Danny Warren might need to be dealt with like his father."

"Donahue, Martin was my friend."

"Cut the bullshit, because I'd hate to see how you'd treat an enemy. Now is it a deal." The men shook on it, making the deal final.

PARTY TIME:

Cool James was performing at the Tunnel night club, The Decons were in the Tunnel over 100 deep and King James had been trying to catch Cool for two years, just because of his name. Several times in Queen's Cool James had narrowly escaped, but King James knew tonight it was on. Cool James wouldn't get away. Even Adrian flew up for the weekend. Adrian had been getting so much money under the table for endorsements; he purchased four Cadillacs, all under 10 gees a piece at the time. After rolling to the party in class, Decons locked down VIP, at the time Queens and the Bronx was going through a feud between major rappers M.C. Shan and KRS-One. Still Boogie Down Production and the Juice Crew All-stars were in the place. There was too much tension in the air.

"Is Brooklyn in the House?" The crowd went crazy.

Cool James was finally on stage; King James rushed the stage followed by 30 goons. They all stood there, no movement, just watching the stage. It was easy to see something was about to go down. Bystanders crept off slowly. Now from the other side of the club, BDP surrounded. Adrian and Danny were at the table watching. It started with L.P. jumping on stage with a champagne bottle hitting Cool's Deejay and snatching his necklace, which set off a chain reaction. King jumped on stage followed by 20 some odd goons. He attacked Cool, slamming him on stage. He began to pummel the young rapper. BDP and Juice Crew began fighting, the melee poured out into the street. There were at least 40 fights going on at once. By now, Adrian and Danny were also in the middle. It was hectic, even women were getting beat up by men. The questions asked.

"Where are you from", the wrong answer got your ass kicked.

As police and ambulance arrived, so much shit was going on. EMS crashed a few times, over fifty people were arrested, among them Adrian Walker. Front page news and of course the media made Adrian out to be the bad guy. Also second page news, a woman walking her dog in central park, found a man floating face down in the Westside Lake. Police have already said it was foul play, as the 25-year-old Ernesto Arroyo was said to have over $2000 dollars in his pockets and all his jewelry still intact.

Bakemen sat in his office with Charles Jefferson, William Bradshaw's father in-law.

"Please sir would you like a cigar", Bakemen offered,

extending the case holding the $1500 a piece Cubans.

"Don't mind if I do, my wife doesn't allow me to enjoy things I use to."

"Well, Mr. Jefferson, I hear you use to be an investment banker."

"Yes, please Attorney General, call me Charles."

"And you call me Harper."

"Alright, Harper", Charles said taking a toke on the cigar.

"I use to invest in small businesses, mostly Midwest."

"Ah, so you understand the importance of organization."

"Of course Harper."

"That's what I've been trying to explain to your son in-law, but he's so stubborn Charles" "Harper, you have to understand where the boy comes from, he was raise in the projects, by two hard working parents that both worked two jobs and were barely home. So that left their three children home alone to run the streets." Charles paused to take a pull off the Cuban.

"While his parents worked, the oldest child, a boy named Phillip began selling dope. Once the parents passed a year apart, Phillip took care of both siblings, shit Phillip even paid for William to go to school." Once the parents passed a year apart, Phillip took care of both siblings, shit Phillip even paid for William too go to school."

"Out of his dope money", Bakemen asked.

"Yes sir, isn't that the fairy tale ending." Both men laughed.

"So you said two siblings."

"Yeah, there's a girl somewhere, last I heard from my daughter she was in a rehab, but that was over three years ago."

In less than an hour, Bakemen had all the info he needed, they promised to get together soon, maybe a golf date. They shook hands and Bakemen walked him out. Bakemen couldn't wait to get on the phone and call Donahue.

"Commissioner Donahue", he answered.

"Dammit, I know who I called."

"What do you want?" They laughed.

"Bradshaw has a heroin dealing brother", before Bakemen could finish Donahue had answers. "Phillip 'Flip' Bradshaw doing life in Otisville and a beautiful sister, well at least she uses to be before crack hit so hard, Monica. I fucked her couple times, she works for Ray Roberts."

"You mean to tell me you knew all this and said nothing.

Joey, I got my nigger."

Once again both men laughed. This was a cut throat game, and blackmail was the greatest weapon.

No one knew where Frenchy was, but there was a key and a half missing, Bobby was flipping. "Dammit, while you're running around partying, this crack head motherfucker done robbed me for everything."

Danny sat there with his head down, but L.P. was tight. He hated the way Danny let Bobby talk to him.

"Danny, I love you. I love you. I loved your father but this shit is on you, you gotta handle this one. I want this motherfucker dead." Bobby slammed the door and left.

"I'm sorry Danny", Mookie said, feeling as if it were her fault.

"Don't worry Mookie, there was nothing you could do", Danny said to comfort her.

"Well, I know what we need to do", L.P. said standing up.

"What's that?"

"Kill that nigga", L.P. said referring to Bobby.

"Shit Mookie, I know you'd ride for us, but you know that niggas an asshole." Mookie nodded.

Danny just shook his head.

"No what, Dee."

"We can't."

"Why not, nigga fuck him."

"He was my pops man, and he the closest thing I got to family, nigga looked out for me, fuck that, we gotta find Frenchy."

Mookie wanted so bad to say what she knew, but she couldn't, at least not yet. L.P. and Danny jumped into Danny's 300 Benz; they rode up and down the streets looking for Frenchy.

"You ever think about your Pops", L.P. asked.

"For what?"

"You never thought about goin to see him or nothing?"

"For what Lance?"

"Cause he's your father and regardless of the past, he loved you."

"How the fuck, do you know that?"

"Because he stayed Danny, damn. I never had a father. My dad didn't love me enough to stay, your dad did. Imagine how many niggas in Brooklyn and here in Harlem don't have fathers and never even had a chance to know them. Your dad was there."

"My dad was never there. I'm 19 years old and couldn't tell you shit about my father, so let's leave the topic alone."

IN DANGER'S EYES

Dope Money to Rap Money:

There was a knock at Williams's office door; he hadn't been home in weeks.

"Alright Sandra, yes I love you, listen someone's at my door." He hung up on her, she also had been pleading for weeks he had.

"Come in", William called out. In walked Stags.

"Oh God, what the fuck do you want, you guys just don't take no for an answer, do you?"

"Whoa, whoa cowboy, slow down, the boss sent me to see if you'd reconsider."

"Tell your boss he could go fuck himself."

"I thought you'd feel that way, you know the thing about crack",

Stags waited for a comment from William, but there was none.

"Well, the thing is the extent these crack fiends will go to, to get high."

Stags now dug into his jacket pocket and pulled out some Polaroid pictures.

"And there sure are some fine black bitches in Harlem that will do anything for this crack cocaine." Stags said, tossing the Polaroid's on Williams's desk.

"And who is this supposed to be", William tried to innocently ask.

"Cut the bullshit Bradshaw, we both know who that is, Monica Bradshaw and boy can she, you know." William took a deep breath and rubbed his temples.

"So what do you want?"

"You, but wait, it gets worse."

Stags now pulled some type of legal documents and passed them over to Williams. They were parole papers for his brother Phillip.

"So as you can see, the balls in your court. It's not so bad; you can make everyone's life easier starting with your own."

That was it, Bakemen now had the Black man he needed on his payroll and all Bradshaw could think was the slave had been purchased. Attorney General Bakemen gave a press conference a week later.

"New York City has an epidemic at hand. Our children are not safe. Our homes are not safe. Our schools and our parks are in danger. Crack Cocaine is like the plague infecting our neighborhoods, but just as Nancy Reagan's slogan is 'Just say no', I agree, but not only do I say no, I choose to fight. We will not let go easy. I tell you drug dealers and you gun runners, we will not just sit around and allow you to destroy our children's futures. No, we say no to you."

Bakemen paused as if he were becoming emotional; taking a deep breath that could be heard through the microphone.

"This is not a war one man can win, no, that's why Commissioner Donahue and I are forming a task force to take our neighborhoods back." The crowd applauded.

"Today is a new day for New York City. Today I appoint one of the city's own, a Harlem native to Head District Attorney, also the First African American DA in New York's history, William Bradshaw."

Everyone including Sandra and her parents were in attendance and they couldn't hide their enthusiasm, the thought of a black man given such power in a time when Harlem was in need of change. Everyone was happy except William.

"Thank you. Thank you…please." William cleared his

throat

, "Ahem, when I graduated John Jay, I had a dream to one day be able to make a difference in this neighborhood. You know the American dream, one man making a difference. Ridding the streets of Harlem, of its bad elements, together we can win this war on drugs."

Bakemen put his arm around Williams shoulder sending chills down William's spine, as camera bulbs flashed.

"Are there any questions", Bakemen asked as hands flew up in the air.

William honestly just wanted to get out of there.

"Mister Bradshaw, after so many years freeing criminals, now you'll be prosecuting the same individuals you just called the bad element."

"Well, unfortunately to reach this level you have to prove yourself worthy on other levels."

"How does it feel to be the first black DA in New York?"

"I pray I'm on the right side." Williams's response almost caused Bakemen to nearly choke.

"Yes, yes we also pray and thank God to have such a fine member added to our team."

Bakemen answered the rest of the questions intended for William, William was obviously uncomfortable. That was the same day of their first staff meeting, William was completely shocked to hear Bakemen and Donahue's first order of business. Their first goal was to shut down New York's Carposi Crime family. After years of rumors that Bakemen worked for the mob, now he was proving the rumors were false. He was taking the mob on. That was the first step in the war on drugs.

1990 was already proving to be a good year; Danny was already sitting on half a million. The Rap game was making a statement, what people thought was only a fad, was looking like it was here to stay. Danny was trying to convince L.P. that was the way to go, the Rap game would be the next big thing. The only thing L.P. was interested in was robbing the New Jewelry wearing neighborhood celebrities and that's all Decon's were known for and Danny was tired of being known for that. Danny and then girlfriend Fame were together at a Poetry reading in Manhattan, that where Danny first met Shawn Turner AKA S.T. Right away, Danny knew S.T. would be a star. The host introduced S.T., a tall slender cat, well dressed out of Brooklyn.

"The Poem I'm gonna read tonight was written by me. It's called These Streets... I got the Daily News Blues some falsely accused path to choose keeps the youth confused, or should I just say the Ghetto, broken glass of 40 bottles lay around the meadows where I grew through the bumps and the bruises the drug abusers the white man for my excuses I won't cry over blood spilled life is too real baby girl using her sex appeal all we know are dark days and cold nights as we hustle till the morning lights haunted by demons of all types hypodermic needles and crack pipes a New York minute gotta move with every second manic depressive since adolescents the streets the only lesson I went to corner of the block college learned to divide product and add cut for a profit a crack head gave me knowledge."

S.T. went on for about 10 minutes; he spoke of broken homes and growing up by himself. Maybe it was the similarity that Danny felt, but to him, S.T.'s words were so powerful. They kicked it at the end; they spoke about him trying to rap. He said he never had, but still Danny volunteered to pay for his studio time, they decided to hook up.

L.P. took care of the business while Danny was busy with his new business venture. S.T. began calling him Danger. They would spend hours in the studio. While L.P. and Bobby hustled and argued, Bobby figured it was time to give up a little fish, so he gave Donahue a call. S.T.'s demo was coming along good, plus the buzz with Decon's was getting him major street credibility. But due to his affiliations, the streets were a little dangerous. He would get several death threats, so Danny was ready to disassociate himself from Decon's, until he could do that it was mandatory that they both be strapped every time they stepped into the street. They had been at Hit Makers Studios down on 36th Street, it was about 3 in the morning, when they got inside the 300 Benz, Danger had brought for S.T., and they were headed uptown. They stopped at a 24-hour Mini Market, which was rare in those days, but S.T. wanted a pack of cigarettes and Danger brought an orange juice.

Danger rolled down the window as S.T. smoked his cancer stick. Danger didn't do anything many nights; Fame had called him a square; he wouldn't even drink a beer. He had his reasons, after the life his parents had led; he wanted no parts of any substance in his body. Whoop Whoop!!! The blue and whites were behind them, they pulled over, really having no choice. "Do you know why we're stopping you? boy", the cop asked S.T.

"Maybe because I'm black, in a better car than you."

"Boy, get the fuck out the car, I smell fuckin marijuana."

That was the reason given they smelled marijuana, although it had been a cigarette being smoked. They found two guns, a 45 on Danger and a 38 on S.T., but only Danger could be charged with gun possession, S.T. was charged with unauthorized operation of a motor vehicle. He had a license for the gun but no license to drive. $10,000 bail for Danger and a $175 fine and ticket for S.T.

Danger would be taken away from the game for a while, it was his second felony, his assault was supposed to be sealed as an Y.O. The ADA used it to convict him as a predicate. It was a sad day when Danger turned himself in to do a 1 to 3 years' sentence. Danger had been home for 3 and a half years, now he was back in Jail. Fame was there every weekend, although he was over 8 hours away in Clinton Danamera State Prison. In those days' prison was gladiator school for real, every day Latin and white boys was cutting someone up and back then a cat might get 60 days, 90 days in the box. It was nothing like D.F.Y., grown men were getting raped. Danger was scared to death, but once men found out his name, he was Decon, and that his father was Showtime Warren, everyone showed love, his father had paved the way for him.

This was where Danger met Benito 'Benny YaYo' Arroyo of the Bronx, the little brother of Ernesto Arroyo, a young man found dead in Central park a year and a half ago. Benny told him the NYPD killed his brother, Benny was now the man, 12 gees a key. Danger came to prison to find a connect that lived 5 minutes away from him. Benny served two years and although Danger had 1 to 3, he'd been hit twice on the board. Benny went home, he sent Danger some pictures of him in the town and it looked like everything he said was true, mad cars and jewels, mad women. So it looked like the connect was real, but Danger kept it to himself, besides L.P. never came to see him but Adrian and S.T. did on a regular basis.

There's Nothing Else:

The biggest game in five years was coming up, Morgan versus Carter, the two most prominent black schools in the country and everyone from ESPN to Sports Illustrated was talking. The match up of Adrian Walker, Morgan's leading rusher, and Damion Jordan, Carter's sack king. Adrian was mad Danger couldn't be there, shit he couldn't even hear it on the radio. They didn't give Black schools airtime back

55 | P a g e

then, but Adrian flew S.T. down first class. The first quarter, Carter went up 10 to 3 and Coach Johnson game plan was to run Adrian the opposite side of Jordan every play, but Adrian was mad although they scored a field goal. Adrian ran for 43 yards in the first quarter while Jordan already had two sacks. Adrian refused to be shown up, Johnson read the play to Quarterback Reign, the team huddled up,

"36 slash back shifted away". Reigns called,

"Break", the team chanted as they lined up.

The play was a run play for Adrian; he was to shift to the opposite side of Jordan.

"Audible",

Reign called once he saw where Jordan lined up, but Adrian didn't move, it looked like confusion on the line.

"Fuck is he doin", Coach Johnson said grabbing his forehead.

"Shift", Reign screamed.

"Same play", Adrian yelled back.

"What's up", the wide receiver to the right called.

"No shift", Adrian screamed, the play clock was winding down.

Reign didn't know what to do, should he call a time out.

"What the fuck?", he turned back and said to Adrian.

"Hike the fuckin ball."

"Shift."

"Hike the fuckin ball." 2 seconds on the play clock.

"Hike."

"Reign drops back five steps, play action, no it's a hand off to Walker, he runs left, spins, breaking a tackle by Willis, stutter steps, cuts in, he's grabbed by Dennis, he's still up, Ooohhh, a crashing blow by Jordan from the blind side, but Walker gains 9 yards", the announcer gave the play by play.

As the players get up, a low moan could be heard under the pile up, as they cleared Adrian was on the ground, his leg is bent in an awkward position.

"Oh, this doesn't look good folks. Adrian Walker is still down, and here come's, the medical staff."

Coach Johnson just stood there with his head down, he couldn't believe what was happening, and he just prayed it wasn't serious. When his team doctor called for the stretcher, he knew it was bad, as they carted Adrian pass Johnson, he couldn't even look at his coach. He had fucked up and he knew it. Morgan went on to lose the game 21 to 17. Damion Jordan was player of the game 4 sacks, 10 tackles, and 2 forced fumbles.

After several x-rays they saw that the knee cap was

shattered, as well as the fibular. No one wanted to tell him, but it was a career ending injury. He lay in Alexi's dorm room, he had received so many get well cards and phone calls. He didn't want to stay in his apartment, it had been two weeks he'd been in the cast and he hadn't gone to any classes. He got the message that Coach Johnson wanted to see him; he drove the 325I to the Coach's office.

"Coach, what's up?"

"Adrian, how you feelin?"

"Good, thanks to these pain killers, I been floatin lately, just waiting to get this cast off so I can get back in the Gym"

Johnson took a deep breath, he sat down, took off his glasses, and rubbed his eyes.

"Adrian." Coach didn't know how to start.

"Listen, the Board of Academics gave me these papers to give you, they'd been looking for you for days, and I figured you were with Alex." Adrian flipped through them,

"What the fuck are these?"

"Discharge papers."

"Discharge; what I hurt my leg and they kick me out of school?"

"Adrian, you had a full sports scholarship."

"Yeah, I'm an athlete."

"If you can't play football, the grant is terminated."

"What the fuck does that mean; this is some fuckin bullshit. I get the cast off in 3 weeks."

"You can't play football anymore."

"Come on Coach, stop playin."

"It's not a game Adrian."

"No, fuck that. I'm playin football, it's a little broken leg."

"No Adrian, the doctor tells me the knee is completely shattered, you may need a replacement." "Fuck the doctors" Adrian was now crying,

"Fuck the doctors Coach, fuck this school, shit, and fuck you."

Coach Johnson jumped up, startling Adrian,

"No Adrian, fuck you. Everybody from day one has been on your ass to pay attention to your grades, especially me, even Alexis, we told you. You have to think past football. You made the decisions Adrian; you decided an education wasn't important. You said fuck what everyone has told you. You said fuck my play, you decided to go left, I designed the play to go right, you said fuck that, so fuck you. You think you're the only one hurt, you broke my fuckin heart kid. Why the fuck didn't you listen?"

Johnson had just realized he had shed tears, he loved this kid, but he had seen it happen to so many hot shot athletes, but the difference with some, was they had an education to fall back on. Tears rushed down Adrian's cheeks. Johnson came around his desk. He hugged Adrian, he knew the kid's story like so many others, but Adrian was going to the pros, there had been no doubt about it. Now he was headed back to the element he wanted so badly to escape.

"What can I do now Coach, what could I do now?"

Johnson couldn't answer that question, no one could. Truth was, at that point and time, Adrian might have been better off dead. Alexis was now going to work and school, taking care Adrian, who moped around feeling like shit.

"Why don't you do something",

Alexis said in a cheerful voice, not wanting to upset him, just trying to encourage him. She was beginning to get depressed herself, watching him be so miserable.

"Do what, what the fuck can I do Lex. All I ever knew how to do was play football. I can't play football no more; I can't do shit."

"Relax Adrian."

"Fuck relax Alexis; I cant't be here no more. I can't take it. I'm goin crazy here, If I stay here I'm gonna die."

"So what, you just gonna pack up and leave me?"

"I love you Alexis. I have never had feelings like I have

for you, but I gotta leave before I go crazy."

"Then I'm goin with you", she said wiping the tears from her own eyes.

"How Lex, school, your job, your parents?"

"Come on Adrian, NYU will definitely accept me, and my parents will just have to understand." So that was it, Adrian and Alexis were headed to New York.

It was 4:15 pm, four vans and eight unmarked cars sat in various different position surround the Island warehouse. Every man eagerly awaiting the signal to rush, this investigation had been going on for over 10 years and finally Donahue himself was sure they'd have enough evidence to get the conviction of his career. He was leading this thirty-man sting and Bakemen assured him this bust would definitely put him in a position with the FBI. The Lincoln Continental pulled into the parking lot of the warehouse, the four men Donahue had been expecting, entered the warehouse. "On my mark, team A and B move around back", Donahue spoke into his Walkie talkie.

Both teams moved into position, A from, the Southside and B from the North. They had fifteen men now positioned and ready to go through the back. C and D teams, five men each, went to the East and West side. While Donahue's team walked right through the front.

"Oh shit the cops",

one of Stagalini's business associates said shielding his

face, unable to do anything else.

"Oh, no problem, he's with us."

"That's where your wrong today Stagalini", Donahue said pointing the gun at Stag.

"Hey, whoa Donahue, Donnie boy, what the fuck gives", Stags plead, not believing what is going on.

"Reginald Stagalini, you have the right to remain silent."

"Donnie what the fuck, c'mon cut the bull", Stags now yelled.

Donahue's team now vegan to grab up the other men and frisk them. Stags still stood there in disbelief.

"You have the right to an attorney", Donahue continued.

"Fuck this", Stags screamed.

"Donahue, I go down, Jimmy will have your fuckin family floating by midnight."

"Who, Jimmy Carposi?"

"Hell fuckin yeah", Stags answered confidently.

"Thank you", Donahue replied, pulling out a tape recorder.

"You fucking cunt Irish pig."

Stag pulled his gun, glass shattered all around them as

teams A through D rushed the premises. This was just the first step in shutting down the New York mob. In hours, Donahue would be slamming the cuffs on Jimmy Carposi himself personally.

There was a week before Danger would be released, after serving 3 years for gun possession. S.T., Fame, as well as Bobby, all awaited his homecoming, but everyone else was leery. L.P. had pretty much fucked up all his money, as well as the relationship with Bobby. Since Danger went to jail, Bobby went from 600 a month, to a little over 200 plus. Bobby was still paying off Carposi, so you could only imagine how happy Bobby had been to hear about the raid on the crime family.

It was 7 pm, March 9, 1990, when over fifty federal agents, as well as Commissioner Joseph Donahue stormed the Whitestone Queens Estate with a search warrant and court ordered arrest warrant issued by Federal Court Judge Archibald.

"What the fuck is this Donahue", Jimmy yelled,

spit flying out his mouth as Donahue began to read Jimmy is Miranda rights.

"Donahue, your dead, you're fuckin dead."

"You're finished in New York Jimmy; we've got enough to put you under Leavenworth." "You got shit, Donahue and you know it." Donahue smiled.

"I got so many witnesses ready to testify, men close to

you, ask yourself who's willing to do the rest of their lives for Jimmy 'the Snake' Carposi?"

Just the idea of men closes to him hushed Jimmy; all he could think of was Stagalini.

"Jimmy Junior", Carposi called his son.

"Yes, dad", the young 10-year-old stood there in tears.

"Straighten up, you're the man now. Come see me as soon as possible."

The agents began to push Carposi out the door. He was arraigned on weapons charges, drug charges, conspiracy murder, murder, conspiracy to distribute, tax evasion, fraud and a slew of other charges. Ordered held with no bail he would be prosecuted by District Attorney William Bradshaw, who was also charging Carposi with everything found in the raid of the Long Island warehouse.

The first visit of course was Jimmy Junior, Carposi's wife Victoria and his Attorney Anthony Cantenelli. Carposi was facing natural life without the possibility of parole; half of his family was in Federal court, the other half in State Supreme.

"Jimmy Junior, I need you to stand up, take over. You have control over the Bronx, Queens and Long Island." That easily, control was passed down.

"Junior, do not conduct my business in the warehouse, discuss nothing in the house on the phone or in the cars.

IN DANGER'S EYES

This is very important I need to see what they have on your father, so please use caution", Cantenelli begged. Jimmy Junior Carposi at 10 years old was the boss.

It was late night, a little after 2 am; King James sat on the Ave. He hadn't slept in two days; he was on a coke binge. He snorted over ten grams in less than forty-eight hours. No one knew about his extracurricular activity, but that's what kept him so amped. He would get high and feel invincible and this night, as he sat in the 535 BMW parked on Flatbush, he was ready to do something. He got out the car, cocked his nine and shoved it in his waist. Wide eyed, sweating, heart pounding; James began to walk the streets looking intensively for a victim. He was so high; he hadn't realized he had been walking for hours. That was when he saw the gray Mazda 626. Whoever was inside the car had their head down. It was a man, he must have been sleeping, and his head was tilted down. James crept up to the driver's side door, he opened it. "Oh, shit", the man inside yelled.

He wasn't sleep at all. James saw the tin foil full of coke.

"Give me every fuckin thing", James yelled brandishing the nine millimeter

"Please take it easy man", the guy pleaded.

"Shut the fuck up and give me everything for I shoot the shit outta you."

The man began to do as he was told.

"That's all", James asked, as the man gave him a couple of dollars.

"Yeah buddy, that's all I have."

"Motha fucker where's your wallet."

"I…I don't have it."

"Motha fucker." Pow.

"Aggghhh", the man screamed in pain.

James shot him in the thigh; James grabbed the foil of coke and began to run.

Blocka, blocka, blocka,

James ducked behind the car as the man began to fire back. The man had, had a gun. James heart raced, he fired back as he began to run again. He ran 30 blocks non-stop back to his car, sixty dollars and another 3 grams of coke, which he sat in his car and snorted right away.

New York's My Dad's and I Want It:

Frenchy would appear every once in a while to rob one of
Bobby's workers, and then disappear. In the three years
Danger had been away, Frenchy had gotten Bobby for over
3 kilos. Although he was rarely found in the hood, Adrian
was back strong, especially his smell for the past few
weeks. He had been working in a pickle factory in the
Bronx and it was clear to Alexis he hated it, but he stuck it
out. Lex and Adrian rented the first floor of a Brownstone
on 143rd; her parents literally were paying for it as she
went to N.Y.U. fulltime. Adrian was more stressed than
ever, but today he tried to hide it. They were outside Gees
Central Station waiting for the man. S.T., Fame and
Adrian, no one else could be found, so this would be his
welcome home, fucked up for a drug king just wait until he
found out he was Broke, Fame sat there quiet as Danger
ranted in a rage,

"Where the fuck is L.P."

"Probably in the hood", S.T. answered.

"Why the fuck ain't he here?" No one had answered.

After three years, most cats are worried about getting their
nuts out the sand, but if you went to jail sitting on 700
grams and came home to 60, there's a lot of other shit on
your mind.

"Niggas is not gonna play me", Danger said turning around

going into his bedroom.

He came back out carrying a briefcase, he turned the dials to the combination numbers and the case snapped open, Danger pulled out two pearl handle 45 automatics.

"These belonged to my father now their mine, just like Harlem, I'm taking back everything that belonged to my dad."

"Please, baby, relax", Fame said, finally breaking her silence.

"Baby what's wrong, you said no more."

"Yeah, of course I said no more. I had almost a million dollars on stash, Niggas took everything from me, my mom's, my dad, six years of my fucking life, now all my money."

He cocked both weapons and tucked them in his waistline.

"So now your just ready to throw everything away?",

Fame asked wiping tears from her eyes, he grabbed her and held her in his arms.

"Fame, I love you, you might be the only one I have ever loved and I promise you no more jail, but no one will ever take shit from me again. S.T., get the car."

"Where we headed?"

"To take back New York." Danger meant every word he

said.

Adrian had to pick up Alexis but promised to page Danger as soon as he got back uptown. First things first, Bobby Rich.

"Oh my fucking God. Son."

Bobby Rich jumped to his feet when he saw Danger walk into the ex-number spot, now an ice cream shop. Bobby walked over and hugged Danger. Danny accepted the embrace, but there was no love in his heart at the moment.

"When you get home?"

"Today."

"Oh, man is it good to see you", Bobby added.

"What's up with this shit", Danger asked, gesturing to the Ice Cream Shop.

"Oh, the stinking pigs done shut down the number game, all we got is crack now, so you ready to get down for me", Bobby said with a smile.

"Bitch, where is the money?" Danger now exposed the guns on his waist. Bobby swallowed heavy,

"Ah, Danny, come on in back, let's talk."

Bobby was scared to death; he'd seen Danger kill with his own eyes.

"What troubling you Danny?"

"When I left, I had over a half million, now I got shit", Bobby now relaxed a little.

"Man, a lot of shit went down, young Blood, while you were gone the kid will tell you", Bobby said pointing to S.T.

"That pig Donahue has been squeezing me so hard, plus Frenchy been robbing me every chance he gets and your boys done ran 125th and 139th into the ground."

"Is that true S.T.", Danger asked. S.T. nodded.

"I want what's mine; you hear me Bobby? Harlem is mine. All you motherfuckers owe me and I want it, so be prepared because all of you better pull rabbits outta ya'll asses. Let's go S.T. Bobby, I want 200 gees by Friday, you got 48 hours."

S.T. and Danger walked out, that quickly Bobby had caught a massive headache, and he rubbed his eyes, picked up the phone and dialed the number.

"Ah, Joe there's a problem."

"Yeah, what the fuck is that?"

"Warren's home talkin bout he wants what's his."

"Ha, ha, that sounds like your problem Bobby, not mine."

"What should I do Joe?"

"Give em what's his", Joe hung up.

Bobby knew he was by himself on this, he just held the receiver in his hand as the busy signal screamed.

"Right here, park",

Danger told S.T. as they pulled up on 169th Street and Clay Ave.

There was a small restaurant on the corner, Jim's Café and right next to it was a Barbershop, just as he had been told Cut Masters. Both Danger and S.T. walked inside, it took a second but they did. Danger spotted who he was looking for, 'Benny YaYo' Benito Arroyo; he was tight up in the corner with some young Spanish chick.

"Oh shit, adios M. Moreno", he jumped up.

"Oye a fuckin celebrity, this is Vinny, Vinny you know who this is?" Vinny shook his head no, everyone turned to face the Black man, Benito was making such a fuss over.

"This is Showtime's son", Benny answered.

"The Showtime", an older barber asked.

"Yes, Martin Showtime, finally amigo you come to see me."

It still shocked Danger how everyone reacted to his father's name, he was beginning to have a change of heart about his dad.

"Yeah Benny I just got out today, can we talk?"

Benny could tell this wasn't just a what's up visit, so he took Danger and only Danger into the back office. When they walked in, the first thing Danger saw was the barrels of weed, at least seven all filled to the top with the green plant, the smell was so strong it made Danger screw up his face.

"So Papi, you really don't smoke?"

"Or drink", Danger added.

"So what's good Papi?"

"You heard of my father." Benny nodded.

"Well, New York was his and I want it and I know you can help me."

"What can I do?"

"I need the connect, you said you had it and I need it."

Benny sat there for a moment just pondering; he knew this would be either his biggest and best mover or his downfall. There wasn't too much loyalty in the Blacks, shit Nelson Brooks showed it, rumor had it from one person he had told on Showtime and honestly Benny thought to himself Showtime may have been the last of the honorable men it the hood, but he was willing to take a chance on Danger. Benny opened his desk draw and pulled out five plastic bags filled with the powdery substance. Each bag had a sticker on it which read Castro.

"This is five kilos of the best coke in New York; I'll give

you a week. It's a key after that; we'll do something for real."

So like that Danger was back on, he already knew where he would be mobbing the drugs. Now he was ready for his team to set back up. So the next stop was Brooklyn.

It was after 10 pm, Danger's first day home and everything had been about business. Now his heart began to pound in his chest, he had done several things today, but this was the scariest. Marcy Project was live and wide awake at this time of night. This was S.T. hood for real. Both men and kids gave him pounds as he walked through, he was the neighborhood superstar. There were a lot of rappers in BK, but everyone knew S would be big. King James and L.P. sat in the middle surrounded by the young thugs.

"Oh shit", L.P. said jumping up, his eyes red from the weed they were smoking.

"My nigga", he added hugging Danger, now everyone followed suit.

"So, the King of New York is home."

"Chill, James, you the King of New York."

"So what's good", James asked.

"Let's walk", Danger said.

The four men walked off, S.T., L.P, King James, and Danger. Already Danger's pager was erupting, this time it was Adrian, I'll get up with you tomorrow Danger thought.

"I'm home and I'm about to literally lock shit down. Fuck what went down while I was gone, it's about right now. Either we gonna get this money or niggas is gonna die broke."

"I'm wit it", L.P. quickly agreed, Danger now looked at James.

"Well?"

"I'm in of course."

"James the stick up shit is dead" Now James sucked his teeth.

"Suck your teeth all you want, but I'm serious that shit is too much heat and we don't need no unnecessary drama, so if you in it's my way or peace."

King hated being talked to like he was a worker, but it was Danger that had him in 325's and 300 E's, so he had no choice but to rock, he nodded.

"So tomorrow everybody meets me at Mookie's house."

That was it; the 5-man team was back on. Now all Danger hoped was Bobby Rich was ready to bow out peacefully, if he wasn't, fuck him. It was a new day and them old niggers was finished.

None of the Carposi crime family had seen each other. Reggie Stags had been held for forty-eight hours. Now they had him in Manhattan Tombs waiting to see a judge, he was pissed. A detective approached the holding cell.

"Reggie Stagalini", he asked.

"Yeah, what the fuck do you want?"

"Come with me", the cop said, opening the cage.

"Put your hands behind your back." Stags followed the order and began to walk.

The cop led him to a room with a bench,

"Sit down."

Stags sat down, he heard the door lock behind him, there was a mesh window with a bench on the other side. The door opened and there stood the 6 foot 1 inch, 210-pound frame.

"Oh god, not fuckin you, the most powerful Moolie in Harlem."

"Yeah, fuck you too Stagalini", William Bradshaw replies.

"What the fuck are you doin here?"

"Well Stags, you tell me, you're the one that forced me into this position."

William sat back, pulled out a cigarette and passed one through the wire window to Stags. "Listen Bradshaw, it was Bakemen that wanted you, I was just doin my job." William laughed. "Now look how the tables have changed, now it's you and Carposi, Bakemen wants and I'm getting paid to do the job and the same men that got you to fuck with my life are paying me to fuck with yours."

Now Stags facial expression changed.

"Don't look so shocked. If Donahue made the arrest, who do you think gave the order." Stags slammed the palm of his hands on the desk.

"Fuckin Bakemen."

"Ah, you're not as dumb as you look Stags, now here's the deal, you give up Carposi and you walk out of here free, maybe even the head man rather the number one Capo."

"Tell Bakemen to fuckin blow me."

"C'mon Stags, I mean do you really have a choice, either you rot or Jimmy does and Stags you know as well as I do Carposi's not gonna sacrifice his ass to save yours."

Although Stags was silent, he wasn't even considering ratting on his boss, Stags was loyal and as long as he kept quiet, they had only what was in the warehouse.

"I'll die before I dishonor my family", Stag finally stated.

"Oh, you'll die alright, who do you think Carposi's gonna be pointing the finger at?"

"Are you crazy Bradshaw, Jimmy knows better than to think some shit like that." Now William shook his head no.

"Tsk, tsk, tsk, maybe, but when your released free of bail and no charges pending, even the Jersey families are gonna be suspicious and you know Jimmy Junior is in charge now."

"What do you mean no charges? What the fuck are you talkin about Bradshaw?"

"Bakemen doesn't need you. We have everything to convict the entire Carposi family, including you, but both Bakemen and Donahue want to make it a little more interesting and letting you go does just that."

"Fuck you Bradshaw. You've got nothing, fucking nothing, your bluffing and I've got just as much dirt on Donahue as he's got on me."

"Yeah he knows that, that's why he's putting you on the streets, if you survive Jimmy's wrath, you deserve to live."

Now William dug through his papers and pulled out one sheet and passed it through the window slot.

"What's this?"

"This is just to show you I'm not bullshitting you, it's your indictment papers."

Stags eyes were wide open now as he read the indictment, he was only charged with trespassing. "Fuck you Bradshaw", he said jumping to his feet.

"Fuck you, fuck Bakemen, and tell Donahue fuck the cunt he crawled outta."

Two court officers now ran in to subdue Stagalini.

"You hear me Bradshaw, tell Donahue fuckin blow me."

Stags calmed down as he walked into the courtroom with his hands cuffed behind his back, the first thing he saw was Teets sitting in the first row with a badge around his neck. After 5 years together, Teets turned out to be a Federal Agent. It's almost impossible for a man to explain that feeling. It's like you can't swallow, your throat is dry like the desert. It closes up on you, you can't speak and your heart skips a beat causing a slight pain followed by hollowness, then you realize they've got you because the motherfucker has been there every step of the way. This coward motherfucker knows every move you've made in the last five years, that's all you can think, this coward motherfucker. Still the feds were no closer to Carlos.

They Denied Jesus:

Benny YaYo was officially the connect, he had raw. Uptown, word on the street was Danger's shit was so raw, it cooked itself. And one by one, danger took over Bobby's blocks, but out of respect Danger still gave bobby 25 gees a week, which was hardly enough to cover Bobby's bills with Jimmy 'the Snake' locked up. Now Jimmy Junior had his hand in Bobby's pockets, Jimmy Junior was more of an asshole than his father had ever been and was quickly letting it be known that he was the boss of the New York family and regardless of what had happened before the mob wasn't going without a fight and Jimmy Junior was ready for war.

Danger was back in the music business. S.T. had an album complete and they tried desperately to shop it, but none of the major labels was signing him. S.T. was quickly getting discouraged. There was still money on the streets but Danger knew it didn't last long. So he was determined to make it in the music industry. They booked show after show, and would literally throw knots of money into the crowds, it became their trademark. I-ACOCA records as half the hood bumped S.T.'s underground album "Make

Moves".

'You cats don't know nothing about Money Machines or triple Beams or Jet Ski's in Caribbean Seas, ya'll sippin Malibu's while I'm sittin in a Malibu breeze'.

He was the hottest thing rapping; he just couldn't get a major label to pick him up. Cell phones had just gotten big, 1991 the big brick phones. Danger and S.T. were sitting in City Hall with city officials trying to get permits to shoot S.T.'s first video. Danger was paying out his own pocket, when his phone rang. Even the politician in City didn't have cell phones yet and here was this young well groomed, well dressed, young black man sitting in the office.

"Yeah, yes", he sucked his teeth.

"C'mon, yeah I'll see what I could do, let me call you back."

S.T. could see that Danger was pissed and to make matters worse the officials shot down the permits. They walked out of City Hall pissed. S.T. was a little leery, but still he asked,

"Who was on the Jack?"

"D-Most."

D-Most was one of the biggest producers in New York, the name had S.T. excited.

"What'd he wants", S.T. asked.

At first Danger just shook his head, S.T. was worried could it be D-Most wanted to sign him, but then it donned on him Danger wasn't a selfish dude like that, if it had been good news Danger would have told him right away. Still S.T. didn't want to push the issue, but Danger was more than his manager and producer, he was his man.

"Hell, Danger what's good?"

"This nigga King James, man he robbed Budda Bless and took his chain."

"Budda Bless out of Queens Bridge?" Danger just nodded,

Budda Bless was the youngest and hottest rapper in the game, to take his necklace would be starting a war. Budda had people just as dangerous on his side, but D-Most was trying to keep it from escalating.

"So what we gonna do about it", S.T. asked.

"About what?"

"Everything." Danger's smile was like the grin of the Devil.

"We gonna shoot our video, get Buddha's chain back and your gonna write the song about it, this is it. Nobody's gonna help us, so it's time for us to do what we gotta do."

IN DANGER'S EYES

"I'm sick of this shit", Adrian yelled.

"Relax baby."

"Everything is fuckin relax with you Lexus. I'm sick of smelling like fuckin pickles, eyes burning from getting pickle juice in them, my skin starting to turn green. I'm done with this shit."

Adrian walked out the door, slamming it behind him. Although his anger had nothing to do with Alexis, she always would be on the receiving end of his rage. Adrian jumped in his raggedy 325I and headed to the Lime Light, a rinky dink bar on 8th Ave. He sat at the bar, and took shot after shot of whiskey. After about 8,

"Damn, I was gonna ask you to buy me a drink, but maybe I should buy you one."

Adrian looked up to see a fine dark skin sister with a body like whoa.

"If you buy a drink, I'll buy dinner."

"Deal", Chocolate answered, that was the night Adrian met Jessica Lee.

Alexis was worried sick, so she paged Danger, who paged Adrian.

"Dammit man, Lexus is worried sick, where are you?"

"Lime Light."

"On 8th?"

"Yeah."

"What the fuck are you doin at that rat hole?"

"I just needed to get out."

"Don't move, I'm on my way." Danger walked in 10 minutes later.

"Danger Jessica, Jessica Danger."

"Oh my god, your Daniel Warren."

"Yeah and this is Adrian Walker, what's the big deal?"

"Wait a minute, you Adrian Walker?" Adrian smiled and nodded.

"When were you gonna tell me"

"Chill ma, listen Ad, we shootin a video tomorrow, so be ready by 10."

"In the morning?"

"Yeah."

"Where?"

"BK and Harlem."

The following morning Danger picked Adrian up from Jessica's house.

The 5-man crew was all together again. That was the first time Danger pulled out the 600 Benz, he had on the mink and all his jewelry and although King James knew he had to give it back, he sported Budda Bless's necklace. This was the picture that stared Grandpa's story, it was also this day the video started on Eastern Parkway. There were crowds of young girls and thugs' eager to be in the video. As S.T. ran through his song, AD, Danger, L.P. and James posted up like the gangsters they were.

"What you know Beamers and Acura's no actors you want dough get at us stashers and stackers BK known for Gun Clappers, killer nothing less, he's King James it ain't hard to tell why he got B, bless on his chest, why ya'll hating on the S, I could see ya anger but before you try to test remember uh oh Danger."

It was almost 1 pm when the first part of the video was done, due to police interference, someone called the police. When the police arrived, a riot almost broke out, as police grabbed King James; he was being placed under arrest. A cop identified him as a man that shot and robbed him six months ago, the scene was hectic. Not only did thy not have permits, but now James was being arrested for the attempted murder of a cop. District Attorney Hollis set bail at one million. When the crew refused to bail King James out, he flipped. He knew Danger had to have the money, but honestly he didn't. Drugs were being sold, but anger was putting everything in S.T. production. While James was getting ready to fight his case, I-ACOCA Records continued to shoot S.T.'s video in Harlem. Danger paid for the four of them to fly to the islands for the shoots.  He rented a 50foot yacht, a few speed boats, jet skis, a mansion and several of the Islands hottest women, altogether he spent 400 gees out his own pocket.

Bobby was scared to death when he heard Jimmy Junior was coming to see him.  Bobby was probably the richest man in Harlem, but always screamed broke and now with Danger home taking over Harlem, it was the best thing that could have happened, and he used that to his advantage.

"So once again Bobby you don't have shit for me huh?"

"Man Junior It's that fuckin Warren kid, your dad knows about him."

"I don't give a fuck about Warren or his fuckin kid, I want my fuckin money."

"But he's got Harlem; and taken everything for years.  I controlled these streets, now I'm here selling fuckin Ice Cream.  You help me, I'll help you."

"So what's going on with this Irish pig Donahue?"  Bobby just shook his head.

"You set up a meeting with this Daniel Warren?"

"What if he doesn't want to meet?"

"Bobby, Bobby, Bobby, you know its bout to be hell up in Harlem, and the more niggas dead, the better, Carlos isn't playing."

For weeks, Junior had been looking for Reggie Stags, but it was as if he'd disappeared off the face of the earth. He couldn't be found anywhere and hadn't been seen by anyone. Junior had every source even certain police that were still on his payroll. Stag hid out in the SoHo area of New York and Rockland County. For years Rockland had been a hideout for gangsters, even Dutch Shultz had hidden there from the feds. Anyway Stags knew there was a price on his head, he had lost everything and was honestly trying to find a way to get it all back. His houses were seized and of course being watched, his bank accounts frozen and with Teets being a Fed. He honestly had no one he could trust; one thing he knew was he wanted Junior dead. Jimmy 'the Snake' wasn't even a worry, the Feds would put him under the ground. Stags was headed out to Connecticut to see his mother, who was battling breast cancer.

Jimmy 'the Snake' had lost quite a bit of weight, he looked horrible but Junior would never tell him that.

"So what's goin on?"

"Still no Stags dad and once again Bobby has nothing for me, Giano gave 150 for Queens, the Baldwin Brothers when they're doin good over 300, Yonkers forget about it."

"So Bobby's given problems."

"Yeah, he says something bout Warren's kid."

"Showtime"

"Yeah, his son's takin everything, Bobby said you know

about em."

"Yeah set up a meeting with him."

"Done it already." Jimmy 'the Snake' smiled, his boy was born to be a boss.

"Good Junior, the Moolie probably needs a connection; him buying from us is as good as him workin for the family."

"Good idea Dad, and Stags?"

"His mother lives in Hartford, but Cantenelli says he's disappeared and the DA hasn't been able to find him, so fuck em, he'll get his."

"Dad, he deserves to die."

"Junior, Stags was the best man at my wedding, he's your godfather, he's a good man, leave him alone, he'll get what he deserves."

Junior heard his father's words but he couldn't believe them, maybe it was the medication, it was because a man his father was sitting in prison. How could his father sit there rotting in a cold cell and not want the man dead, no not at all. Junior couldn't let it go so easy.


Step Up to the Plate:

The crowd cheered, it was definitely a reason to applaud.

The past four years had showed so much change. The man who had almost single handedly taken down the Mafia in New York had just been elected Senator of New York.

"Ladies and Gentleman I give you, your New, New York Senator, our own Harper Bakemen." The crowd erupted to applauses that had to go up at least 4 or 5 more decibels. Bakemen was a savior to some, truly a man fighting strong in the war on drugs.

"Thank you, thank you, please, thank you." Bakemen loosened his tie,

"I've been here before standing in front of you, I've made promises and now I ask have I delivered?" The crowd cheered loudly, agreeing with the Senator.

"Now I stand here again with a different rank, we've shut down the Carposi Crime Family, we've shut down the Arroyo Cartel, and we put an end to Nelson Brooks and the Black Death."

The crowd seemed mesmerized and as Bradshaw sat in the background, he couldn't help but think what about you Bakemen, the biggest dope dealer of them all.

"Today I have a new plan, look around, what do you see?" Everyone looked around, confused. "Do you see what I see, do you? Well, I see a drug free Harlem. I see the home of Jazz. I see the home of black pride. I see a people that shouldn't have to live in fear. So today is the beginning of Plan B, Today I appoint District Attorney

William Bradshaw to Attorney General. William almost choked at a time when he should have been excited. He was pissed.

"Yes, and we'll be moving our offices right here to Harlem, right here in the Adam Clayton Powell Building."

Flash bulbs exploded as they took pictures of both Bakemen and Bradshaw. The Jefferson's were elated.

"What's wrong baby",

Sandra asked as she wrapped her hair in a bun, so she could prepare herself for bed.

"You should be so excited; do you know the money you will be making now."

Everything was money for Sandra and her parents, but not so much for William.

"There are other things to life than money."

"Yeah, name one William."

"My soul", he answered.

"Ha, ha", Sandra laughed snobbishly.

"Can your soul pay our mortgage; I have never seen you play the saxophone William dear."

It was senseless talking to her but William had plans of his own. Teets whose real name was Howard Marshall was set to testify this week on Jimmy Carposi, maybe his testimony would be able to convict or incriminate more than just Carposi. Maybe this was the best thing that could happen to him. He was now in a position to make a difference, he had his own plans.

There was a knock at the door.

"One minute",

the old woman called as she made her way to the door, she didn't move too well. She thought about the days when the house had been full of children, the bell rang again.

"I'm coming", she called out again. She answered the door.

"Okay can I help you", she asked.

"Yes, Miss Stagalini."

"Yes."

Stags rushed to Westchester he knew who had done this and he also knew they would be there to watch him. Still Reggie's imagination was driving him crazy as he thought about what he would arrive to see at the scene of his childhood home. What had he done, this life he had chosen, his father was probably turning in his grave right now in disgust of what his oldest son had become. Italians didn't have it easy when arriving to America, the Dutch and the Irish gave them hell. They were discriminated on them just like the blacks and the Jews. Stags dad came to America in the late 1930's, a young man of 15, no education trying his hardest not to fit the stereotype all Italians were mob and mafia related. He worked in a shoe factory to support his family. Vincent Stagalini died working, so his family wouldn't be looked upon as the scum of Italy and that is just what his son had done. Now it was biting him right in the ass.

Stags arrived to fire trucks, police cars, as well as, an ambulance. The house was just a charred frame; his mother lay on the gurney, her face and clothes covered in black and gray soot. As she cared about her heirlooms that she had lost in the fire the old woman had taken a beating but that hadn't mattered to her. She only cried for Vincent Reginald Stagalini's belongings, Stags tried to comfort his mother who began to blame him, that's when Stags saw Junior's henchmen in the Caddy. Tony Cheeks and Andy Fatts then drove off. Tony blew a kiss to Stags, who in return gave him the finger. It wasn't over, shit it was far from over. There would be hell to pay. Junior was damn near by himself and he had started a war, one that Stags knew he wasn't ready for.

Charlene awaited her man's verdict. Adrian, L.P. and S.T. were also in the audience. Officer Polanco tested positive for cocaine and was suspended, but King James was still on

92 | P a g e

trial for shooting the officer in the leg and robbing him. It had taken a little over 45 minutes for the jurors to find a verdict. James lawyer's defense was that under the influence of cocaine it was possible that officer Polanco didn't know who robbed him the night of the incident. He went to the hospital and never once said anything about being robbed and it was obvious it had worked. The jury found King James not guilty on all charges, he was a free man and quickly his legend was growing. James felt untouchable; he had shot a cop point blank range and had walked out as the King of New York.

Across town in a Manhattan court, a hearing was being held on behalf of James 'Jimmy the Snake' Carposi. His lawyer Cantenelli had just filed a motion to dismiss for lack of evidence. Bradshaw was going crazy; no one could locate field agent Teets. Carposi just sat patiently at the desk with a smug little grin. Jimmy couldn't possibly walk out of that court room a free man, with no key witness, he would. The only thing William would be able to charge the Snake with, would be tax evasion, a two-year term. Bradshaw's phone rang, it sounded like the chime of Bib Ben in the drop dead silent courtroom.

"Yes", Bradshaw said.

"Yes, you're kidding me, unbelievable, alright."

William hung up his cell phone. Jimmy's grin was now a full-fledged smile.

"Your honor, the people ask for a half hour recess."

The judge granted it. Donahue's men had found Teets floating face down in his own bathtub, there was Bradshaw's witness

Danger wouldn't meet anywhere else but the Bronx neutral ground. The meeting took place on 169th and clay, two stops down from Benny YaYo's Barbershop, in a small restaurant, Jim's Café. The meeting was between Junior, Danger, and Benny. Right away Danger was shocked to see how young Junior was. Now he knew why his nickname was Baby-faced Junior

"Finally somebody with a little youth", Junior said extending his hand.

Danger accepted right away. Danger saw the differences between Junior and the Snake. The Snake wore fine suits, linen, silk, shark skin. Junior was there in a jogging suit and sneakers. The Snake wouldn't be caught dead in a running shoe, his shoes alone cost a gees a piece. They sat at a table in the back; Junior had two goons sitting at a table next to them.

"So, Danny what's goin on in Harlem?"

"Nothin much, getting ready for the Ruckus Tournaments. I got my own team."

"Oh yeah, what are they called?"

"The Ghetto boys." Junior nodded his head in approval of the name.

"So, how you makin a living?"

"Well, I'm trying to get my record label off the ground."

"Oh, so you're a Rappeeerrr", he said in a funny way.

"No, I'm a producer. We're making money doing shows."

"Cut the bullshit Daniel."

"What bullshit James?" Junior laughed at that for a second then his face quickly got serious.

"You think this is a game, Bobby told me everything, I know your controlling 116th to 139th and I want in."

"You sound like your father."

"Yeah. Well, I'm taking over his business."

"Well you see where he is."

"What the fuck does that mean?"

Junior jumped up causing a scene, patrons turned to watch what was going on.

"Relax, Junior I'm just saying sometimes a mans greed can be his own downfall." Junior now smiled. "Also a man's friends can be his downfall, I'm sure your father has told you that", It actually went right over Danger's head.

"Look Daniel, I didn't come for arguments, I came to talk business, and I mean we could be partners." Danger just shook his head.

"You're saying no; you haven't even heard me out."

"I don't need any partners."

"Listen, I have great product. I can give you beautiful prices."

"Oh, yeah. Let me see your product."

With a hand gesture, one of his goons brought over a suitcase. The whole idea made Danger smile, Junior must have just known that Danger was gonna jump on his team. The goon pulled out a Ziploc of cocaine and tossed it on the table.

 Danger looked at the dull white powder, he opened the bag and smelled it, and he screwed his face.

"Do you sniff", Junior asked.

 "No, do you?"

 "I do a little line or two, every now and then", Junior replied.

"So, what's this?"

"Half a key", Junior answered.

 "So how much for this?"

"9 gees."

Danger smiled and shook his hand; he reached into his waistline and pulled out his own package of cocaine.

"Junior, do you see the crystals in this, how it shines?"

Danger dug in his pocket, pulled out a 10 gees stack and tossed it to Junior, he then took Junior's bag and pound it inside his own and shook the two substances up mixing them together.

"I needed a cut for this, want to try it?"

This offended Junior, he grabbed the gun off his waist and placed it on the table at the same time both his goons exposed their weapons, this got no reaction from Danger.

"Junior, think about it, look around you."

"Do you think I give a shit about these niggers and spies in here", Junior whispered.

"No, of course not, neither do I. I'm one of the biggest crack cocaine dealers in New York; I could care less about any bitch in here, but look. Look at the counter, both ends." Junior looked. "Yeah to the two Spanish dudes, look at the two tables by the door and the two by the rest room. Maybe you should put the guns away and just walk out. Whenever I need some cut, I'll give you a call. Ha, ha, ha, ah, get the fuck outta here", Danger said, almost unable to control his laugh. "Yeah, I'm leaving but watch your ass Daniel, everybody around you can't be trusted. You and I will talk again."

"Yeah, we'll talk when I need cut, oh and keep the change."

Junior walked out pissed, he had been embarrassed in front of his henchmen and he was determined to get the respect he felt he deserved. Tony Cheeks and Andy Fatts had already fucked up one order he had given and he felt they disobeyed him due to a lack of respect. Junior wanted Stags 80-year-old mother dead and they had spared her life.

"Tony find the closest person to Danny Boy and kill them"

"Yes, Boss", Tony Cheeks answered.

"Tony."

"Yeah, Boss."

"Kill Them."

"I got it." With that they head to Long Island, a shipment had come in that needed to be counted.

"Joseph, it needed to be done. I promise you everything will be fine." Donahue felt fucked up, he had betrayed Jimmy 'the Snake'. Bakemen didn't give a fuck; Jimmy had been a pawn, a sacrificial piece. The feds had been watching his movements, so Bakemen had to give them a bust to get them off his back, but even he didn't know that Teets had been a federal agent. "Dammit, are you on a secure line?"

"Yes", Donahue answered Bakemen.

"Teets had been taken care of, he's no threat, and I promise you. Now just relax. I have two tickets to the Cayman Islands; take a vacation, maybe a nice week or two could do you some good." Donahue took a deep breath,

"I can't. I have this whole Polanco situation to deal with."

"Do you realize; in two weeks I will be sworn in as New York State Senator? The Dominguez brothers are ready to give almost a billion dollars in product, right now is the wrong time to let your conscious get the better of you. Just talk to Jimmy Junior Get him under control."

"How do I do that, after I locked up his dad?"

"The boys an asshole. Convince him it was all Teets fault and he's young, money will easily persuade him. Offer him a Benz or something. Just stand up man. I need you to be strong on this one dammit. I'll call you in two days, have some news for me."

Bakemen hung up, he knew he had made a mistake when he talked to Showtime that night, but O'Mayer's had gotten too cocky, too ambitious. So Bakemen promised Showtime more power than the police commissioner himself if he'd get rid of O'Mayer and Showtime did just what Bakemen had wanted.

Bakemen picked up the phone and dialed the number, so all those years ago Showtime had been expecting everything to go how it went. But it was Bakemen that was reneging on the deal, the phone rang twice.

"This is Junior"

"Junior, Bakemen here."

"Senator, what can I do for you?" The Devil's grin came across Bakemen's face.

"We'll I've done your father a big favor, now I myself need a huge one" Junior knew it was Bakemen that knocked off Teets, why, he didn't know.

"You know it would be almost impossible to say no, but tell me what's in it for me."

"My God Junior, I'm already making you a rich man, but how bout two tickets to the Caymans." Junior laughed.

"Yes, that's good, what is it."

"Donahue, he's betrayed your father and now he has the Attorney General looking at you." "What", Junior yelled.

"Don't worry, the niggers on his way to my office now. I can take care of him, it's Donahue we need erased."

"Got you." So that was that. So easy, Bakemen could just have a man dealt with; he hung up and dialed another number.

"Attorney General Bradshaw."

"William, its Harper, are you by yourself?" Although he wasn't, he said he was.

"Yeah, what's wrong", William asked.

"Are you ready to really shut these Ginnies down?"

A smirk came across Williams face, because Bakemen

talked about the Italians, he could only imagine the things he's said to them about him.

"Yes, what's up?"

"I'm ready to take down Junior, as well as Donahue. Maybe you should put a tail on Donahue, but tell them do not make a move."

"I got you, Boss", William agreed.

"William, I got two tickets to the Cayman Islands, I know Sandra would like that. They're yours if you get an indictment for me." They hung up,

William was looking for an indictment alright, but Bakemen wouldn't like it, not one bit.

"So, Stagalini that was Senator Bakemen, he wants the same man you do, Jimmy Junior, so what you go for me?"

Budda Bless was the hottest thing in New York, he controlled the air waves and S.T. just couldn't get his break. He got a little airplay, mostly what Danger paid for, but now Danger took no shorts. They had an entire album and paid to press 300 thousand copies. They went to record shops through every borough, to sell them for five dollars a copy. S.T.'s underground buzz was so hot; they sold out in a week. While Budda Bless went Platinum in 3 weeks and took the first Platinum plaque to his projects, but in a week S.T. and Danger had made a million dollars. It was time to step up the game and hit the big studios and get some stars on this next project.

Budda Bless had a performance at the Palladium, S.T. opened for him. S.T. ripped the show apart, the crowd cheered for three encores. Budda was pissed, during his performance S.T. walked on stage, the crowd erupted. S.T. grabbed the microphone and went off, Budda left the stage. The next day, that was all the radio stations talked about. D-Most called in and began disrespecting,

"S.T. is a (Beep) and his man Danger just a reckless (Beep). Them (Beep) lack respect for the Rap game. All they are drug dealers tryin to (Beep) up the Rap Game."

"Whoa, Whoa D-Most chill", Deejay M. Jay interrupted.

"Nah, you got to understand MJ, S.T. ain't even signed to no real label", Budda added.

"Maybe we need to have S.T. and Danger call in. Anybody out there listening to the box have Danger or S.T. call up the station, word up. Defend ya self-dogs, it's on ya'll."

In minutes the phones were blaring.

"This is DJ. MJ, what's the deal, who we got on the line?"

"This is Daniel 'Danger' Warren, ya Heard."

"Danger, what up, have you heard what my man D-Most and Budda Bless been sayin?"

"Yeah, I hear them (Beep) ass (Beep) talkin reckless over the radio."

"Yo Danger, why you and your boy trying steal my shine",

Budda asked, his voice now much calmer now.

"Yo, don't question me, but if NYC wants to know, Budda Bless is a straight (Beep). My team is takin all ya shine, just like D-Most had to call and beg for your jewelry back."

"Oh, snap that was true", MJ asked.

"Yeah, it's true. S.T. raps about what's real. Budda is just a real actor and any of, you cat's disrespect my name or any bodies on my team ever again and we gonna forget about this rap (beep) and hold court on the street" (click).

"Yo, Danger, Yo. You there, oh my God, where ya'll goin, oh snap, ya'll heard it here and check this Budda Bless and D-Most left the building. I repeat Budda Bless and D-Most have left the building."

That was it, S.T. was officially on. The next day, three major labels were looking to sign I-ACOCA Records to a major deal and they were all shot down. S.T. was anxious but this was business and Danger knew if they held out for the right time, they'd get the money S.T. deserved. So he listened to Danger, Danger was rarely wrong.

Serious:

It was a rap, Danger exited the Drug game leaving Adrian in charge. And Adrian handled Business like a G. A lot of shit had gone down lately. Jimmy Carposi was sentenced to 3 years for tax evasion, S.T. and Danger signed with Infra-Red Records, the first album would actually be a remake of the album they had put out themselves and it was already in demand. It was late `92 and shit was popping all over. Alexis had been trying to find Adrian for two days, he was never home. So she had to promise Coach Johnson he'd call him back in a few days. The problem was, after bringing Alexis out to New York, he had honestly fell out of love with her and now loved Jessica Lee. Alexis got in touch with Mookie, who got in touch with L.P., who found Adrian and delivered the message. Adrian called Coach Johnson right away.

"Damn boy, it took you long to get back to me."

"Sorry Coach, I been busy."

"Well, I hope you're in shape, how's the knee feeling."

"Great, why you ask?"

"You're not gonna believe this, but I just got a call from Shula, he wants you to come down to Miami's summer training camp."

"Get the fuck outta here, oh excuse my language Coach."

"Well, I got to get back to him in two weeks, so you take a couple of days, think about it, talk it over with Lexus and you get back to me."

"Yeah Coach for sure. I'll give you a call in a few days."

They hung up.

"Oh my God."

Adrian grabbed Jessica in his arms and twirled her around. He was so happy; he hadn't felt like this in years. His first true love was back, the Dolphins wanted to try him; this was all he'd been waiting for.

"What's up baby", Jessica asked.

"That was my college coach."

"And?"

"And we about to be rich", he said, still holding her.

"The Miami Dolphins want me to come down and try out." She began to push out of his arms. "What's wrong Mami?"

"Huh, we're rich, you mean you and Alexis are rich, I'll just get pushed to the side."

Once again he pulled her into his arms.

"Jessica, are you crazy, I love you. I'll never just push you to the side or leave you."

Once again she pushed out of his arms, now she began to cry.

"Please Jess, don't do this, I need you. I don't love Alexis. It's you I want to be with."

"Yeah, until you find out I'm pregnant." Adrian was stuck; he didn't know how to react.

"See, I knew I shouldn't have told you"

"Jess, we're having a baby?"

"Yes, that's why you can't leave me, not yet, football will always be there."

Would it, would Adrian ever have this opportunity, Alexis didn't think so.

"Are you fucking crazy Adrian? Are you using the drugs you supposed to be selling? "

"See that's the disrespectful shit I be talkin about. You never use to talk to me like that." "Adrian, you're talking mad, this is the opportunity of a lifetime and you're ready to throw it away for the drug game, you disrespecting yourself."

"You don't understand, I have responsibilities, people need me."

"Cut the bullshit. Adrian this is all you ever wanted, this is what you dreamed about as a child. Now you have the chance and if those street corner gangsters can't understand that, then it's obvious their not your friends."

"Listen, my mother's dead."

"And she's probably turning over in her grave." Adrian grabbed his jacket.

"Yeah Adrian, do what you use to do best, run, run away from your dreams. Who would have ever thought I'd come to New York to be with a drug dealing asshole."

Adrian slammed the door behind him.

It was S.T.'s big night, his album release party, everybody was there Mary J Blige, Monica, Shanice and Flex, Heavy Dee, Salt and Peppa, KRS One, Fat Joe, D.I.T.C., Run DMC, Lord Finesse, Ice Cube, Latifah, Anthony Mason of the Knicks, Daryl Strawberry, Doc Gooden, Guy, Spike Lee, even D-Most was there trying to make peace and I-ACOCA had no problems with that. Infra-Red gave them a four-million-dollar advance and Danger spent over 500 gees on the release party alone. This was the biggest event in S.T.'s life. He really wanted to make peace with Budda, but he never showed up.

"Hey Cutie", S.T. turned to see a bad 5 foot 4-inch caramel complexion honey with a bad body. "What up Ma, what's good?"

"You, all this for you", she answered.

"What about that", S.T. asked pointing at her.

"When and where?"

"Shit, right now Ma."

"Lead the way", she said.

S.T. took her by the hand; they went outside, walked around to the alley. He opened the door to his 500 Benz. The woman instantly dropped down to her knees on the dirty ground and began fumbling with his belt and zipper. Once she got it opened, she pulled out his penis and began giving him head. S.T. lay back as she slopped and slopped away, she did this for almost five minutes.

"I Cumming", S.T. let her know.

She took his penis into her mouth deeper, gagging as he came down her throat, she swallowed it all. She then stood up pulling up her skirt as she lay over the hood of the Benz, she moved her panties to the side, and S.T. pushed his unprotected cock in her pussy. She took it out and put it in her ass. It slid in easily, as she moaned as if he were killing her. He thrust in and out of her, his pelvis slapping against her plump ass.

"What's...your...name...name...Ma?"

"Ooh ooh it's...it's, Sharon", she continued to moan.

S.T. came; he really didn't care if she did. He wiped his dick on her skirt, and She laughed.

"We gotta do this again", she smiled.

They both walked back into the party together. D-Most and Danger were actually about to be the two hottest producers in New York. They sat on the balcony talking about money.

"Oh shit", D-Most said in shock.

"What happened", Danger asked.

"Look who your boy S.T. just walked in with."

"Who the fuck is that", Danger asked.

When D-Most Told Danger, he jumped up and rushed to the ground level.

"What the fuck are you doin", he said grabbing S.T.

"Oh, you must be Danger", she said with the same smile that got S.T. in the alley.

"What you mean? I got some pussy."

"Do you know who this bitch is", Danger screamed.

"Please, all that bitch shit ain't necessary", she added.

"Who are you", S.T. asked her.

"Sharon", she said once again with the smile.

"This is Budda's Girl."

"Get the fuck outta here." Sharon nodded

"We tryin to make peace and this is shit you doin?'

"Damn nigga, I thought ya'll was gangstas. I know ya'll ain't worried about Barry", she said disrespecting her own baby daddy.

Danger threw a drink in her face. A little pushing and shoving went on, but it quickly died out. She and D-Most left. At 12 am, over one thousand bottles of Moet popped to celebrate the release of Hot Corner Hustlers, the first of S.T.'s albums. Adrian was drunk as hell.

"Dawg let me holla at you." Danger could smell the alcohol on his breath.

"Damn, you alright?"

"Yeah…yeah man…I'm…I'm good, damn man Jess is pregnant."

"Word, she keepin it?"

"What that mean man?"

"I don't know man, make her have an abortion."

"What, c'mon man, you talkin bout killin my first child man."

"What about Lex, I mean she loves you."

"Fuck Lex, all she cares about is money." "Why would you say that?"

"Cause she flippin cause the Dolphins want me to come down for summer trainin."

"What?"

"Yeah, they called Coach Johnson."

"So when you leavin?"

"I'm not."

"What, are you motherfuckin crazy?"

"Shit, you sound like Alexis."

"Yeah, cause Alexis got some fuckin sense, man this is what you busted your ass for all those years, now you want to throw it all away on some broke hood rat bitch."

"Watch your mouth Danger, that's my Baby Momma."

"Listen man; just think about this before you make the biggest mistake of your life."

Adrian was quiet, as if he were contemplating right then and there.

"I'm not goin, besides who'll take care of business? You busy with this Rap shit, I got drugs to sell."

"Man fuck them drugs." Just as Danger yelled,

the music turned off, everyone turned in their direction, and both Fame and Jessica walked over to their men.

"You ready baby", fame asked, it was after four.

"Yeah, you good Adrian?"

"You know it."

"Look Jess, don't let him drive."

"Now everybody's my fuckin parents", Adrian said, he was drunk as hell. L.P. and James pulled up.

"Where we headed, the Diner", King James asked.

"Nah, I'm headed home", Danger answered.

They all walked out together, giving pounds, hugs and handshakes to other guest.

"S, your whips safe here, get in nigga, you too drunk to drive", King James yelled out, S.T. did just that. Everyone began pulling off.

"So whose Adrian's new chick", fame asked, as she sat in the driver's seat.

Danger began to tell her the events of the night, he told about S.T and Sharon, about Adrian turning down the Dolphins. (Beep) (Beep) Danger turned to see Benny Yayo.

"Mi Amigo Gracias. I had a great time, give me a call, oh shit",

Benny said as the police car pulled up on the driver side of Danger's car, before Benny could pull off, before Danger could say anything, the gun fire erupted. Sparks flew as the bullets hit the metal of the car, glass shattered, Danger passed out. He woke, again he wasn't in his car, and he was lying on the ground.

"Oh shit, oh shit, damn"

"Relax papi", Benny said holding his own shoulder.

"What happened dawg?"

"You got shot."

"Put me in the car son, drive me to the hospital, don't let me die out here, not like this."

"Just be easy", some man Danger didn't know said.

"Just put me in my car."

"No, don't move em", the man said again.

"Bullets might still be inside, you got to be careful."

"Fame....Fame, Where's Fame?" Danger called

"Just lay down, ambulance is on its way."

"Where's Fame." No one wanted to tell him fame was already dead inside his car.

"Yo, I got over 5 thousand in my pocket. Somebody put me in a…car", he passed out again.

June 6 1995, Daniel 'Danger' Warren was shot five times. Fame Anderson was announced dead on the scene. She had been shot over eight times. When Danger awoke in Bellevue Medical Center, the team was there, everyone except Fame. Danger knew what it was; he shed one tear as Benny explained. A year and a half out of prison, Danger had almost died, and lost the only female he had ever been with, the only person he could ever remember loving, they had honestly unleashed a beast. Two white cops could only mean mob related, so Junior had opened a can that could not be closed.

Although doctors objected, Danger signed out the hospital to attend Fames funeral. Her mother blamed Danger for everything and it was true it was his entire fault and he knew it.

"Yo Danger." D-Most approached him, as he sat in the wheelchair.

"What up", Danger answered winching through a slight pain.

"Yo, I had a meeting at Infra-Red. Stan Cohorts offering 10 million if we link up."

"Link up."

"Yeah us, S.T. and Budda, it will be the biggest thing hip-hop has ever seen." Danger thought about it,

"Yeah, well have you spoke to Budda yet?"

"I will, but it's not about Budda, it's about us, you never know, these niggas could just say fuck us tomorrow. Ain't no job security in this shit, we gotta make sure we straight."

That was the first time Danger saw the griminess in D-Most, but it wouldn't be the last.

Father Knows Best

It had been a month since Fame had been murdered; Junior didn't have the slightest remorse for her. He was upset about the failure to eliminate Daniel; this was the second time his henchmen had failed. His father approached the table and sat down.

"So my boy I've been hearing good things about you."

"Yeah dad I'm tryin but these guys are fuckin asses."

"Who?"

"Everyone."

Junior went on to tell his pop about certain events, leaving out the botched hits on Stags mom and the Moolie Warren.

"So Bakemen wants Donahue dead."

"Yeah dad."

"You stay away from that one Junior"

"But dad."

"Stay away Junior do you hear me, stay away and no talk in the house it's not safe"?

Jimmy went on asking questions about the other shit in the street. One of the biggest things legally about the business was alibis. Junior had lost all faith in Tony Cheeks and Andy Fatts, so he hired two Manhattan police officers to handle business for him on the next hit, although his father said no, it was too late. It was being handled as they spoke, Junior just didn't want to tell his dad. The Crown Victoria pulled up to the Queens address, a nice two story single family.

"Oh, Joe's doing well for himself Sonny."

"Yeah Sal, it's Our turn."

Detectives Sonny, Lipsett and Salvatore Beckett got out and walked up to the nice home. As they approach, they could now see the side of the house, a nice 25-foot boat and two jet skis. Yes, Joe was doing excellent for himself. Sonny rang the bell seconds later. Joe's 11-year-old daughter answered.

"Hi little girl, is your dad here."

"Yes."

"Can you tell him Detectives Lipsett and Beckett are here to see him."

Joe's daughter let them in the foyer, she then ran to the den to tell her father cops were at the door, Lipsett and Beck, something at first. Joe was nervous, and then when he saw just who it was, he was more shocked.

"What the hell are you two doin here."

"Sorry Commissioner", Lipsett started,

"but we had some important facts about the Jimmy Carposi Junior Case."

"Oh, oh well, come on in." Joseph led the way to the den.

"Can I offer you guys a drink?"

"Nothing for me sir", Lipsett answered.

"If it's not a bother, do you have any coffee brewing", Beckett asked.

"Yeah, actually my wife was just making some, give me one moment."

Joseph got up to get the coffee for Beckett as the two detectives looked around the den; they paid extra close attention to the photos. There was a family photo, must have been taken last summer, it was Joe, his wife and what they figured to be Joe's three daughters.

"Here you go", Joe said, returning with the coffee mug.

"A Joe, those your three daughters."

"No just the two red heads, the dark haired girl is one of my oldest daughter's friends. They're away together now at summer camp, costing me a fortune."

That was when Joe noticed Beckett had on gloves, it was summertime, something wasn't right. Joe kept a 38 in the draw of his mural; he slowly made his way to it.

"So what's up with Carposi Junior", Joe asked.

Lipsett quickly pulled out the automatic four five with the silencer.

"He wants you dead." Thoooo. Thoooo. Two shots from the silencer and Joe was down.

The two detectives quickly ran through the house killing Donahue's wife and youngest daughter; the hit was complete. They exited the house carefully, eyeing the neighborhood to see if anyone was watching them leave. They got inside the Crown Victoria. Beckett was driving, Lipsett picked up the car phone to dial Junior

"Junior here."

"Boss." Lipsett replied

"Make me smile, tell me My problems gone."

"Yeah boss."

"Good, I sent these two imbeciles to get rid of Warren and Stags and they botched both times, you and me are gonna make lots of money together. I'll give you a call."

Junior hung up, sitting in his living room smoking a cigar, he picked up the telephone again and dialed the number. It rang three times, finally,

"Good afternoon."

"Good afternoon Senator, its Junior Carposi."

"Why are you calling me here?"

"Oh, I just wanted you to know, Donahue's no more."

"You stupid Guinea wop Dago mother fucker, do you know if this is a secure line."

"No."

"Do you even know if your phone is tapped?"

"No."

"Then hang up, I'll call you." (Click)

Bakemen couldn't believe how ignorant, no flat out stupid Junior could be. He had obviously learned nothing from his father's misfortune. It was almost time to get rid of Junior also, within the next year Junior would be expendable. Bakemen inside contact had already schooled him to the fat that Bradshaw had several indictments just waiting to drop on Jimmy 'the Snake'. Bradshaw has even managed to pull Reggie Stagalini out of the woodworks to testify. Bradshaw was just waiting on the right moment as well as Bakemen; he had his own insurance policy just in case Bradshaw got brave. Stagalini testimony could incriminate a lot of people and the first sign of the wrong people, Bradshaw and Stagalini would be floating in the Bronx River.

(Beep, Beep Beep Beep) Adrian pager was going crazy; he needed to get to a phone bad. It was Mookie; she was using the emergency code for every page. He rode shotgun in S.T.'s new 400 LS Lexus.

"Come on man, I need to get to a phone man, you bullshittin."

"Relax, we right here, you might as well just go up there."

It made sense, they were ten blocks away, and it would be a lot easier to just go up to the apartment on 139 and eighth. Mookie hadn't paged in about six minutes after 20 something straight pages. Adrian ran up the stairs followed by S.T. Adrian knocked. It startled Mookie inside.

"Who is it", Mookie called out,

"It's Ad." Mookie struggled with the locks on the door.

"Dammit you, knockin like the police."

"Just open the door, you paging me, like you about to have a baby."

Adrian heard her laugh inside the apartment; she finally got the door opened.

"When ya'll gonna get these locks fixed?"

"Soon Mommie, I promise",

Adrian said entering, kissing Mookie on the cheek, and S.T. did the same.

Now Mookie was far from ugly, shit if you didn't know her, you wouldn't believe she was a crack head. She had a child a few years back that rumor said was Daniel's. For years Daniel had lived with her and many believed Mookie's baby was his but Daniel had made it very clear he had been a virgin until he met Fame.

"So what's so important", Adrian asked.

"Well guess who's in town."

Right away Adrian knew who she was talking about, there could only be one reason for Mookie to page him like that.

"The motherfuckin Frenchy dude." Mookie just smiled and nodded.

"So where's he at", S.T. asked.

"Should be here any minute." Adrian hopped up,

"S let me use your keys." S.T. tossed him the Lexus keys.

"Where you goin?"

"To get Danger." Ad ran out the door,

Mookie locked it behind him. As soon as she turned around, S.T. was right there; he pushed her against the wall and began kissing her.

Once again there was someone banging on the door. Mookie straightened herself up as S.T. went into the bathroom to clean himself up.

"Who is it", Mookie asked.

"Open the door, it's me."

She knew who it was, once again she struggled with the lock, and it finally snapped open. "Dammit what took you so long to open this god damn door?"

"Sorry Frenchy, I have company."

"Oh yeah and I see that cheap ass motherfuckin Bobby still ain't get this door fixed."

"Bobby don't run shit no more." Now S.T. came out the bathroom.

"Who the fuck is you?", Frenchy asked.

"Who the fuck is you?", S.T. responded.

"Please S, this is Frenchy." In one motion, S.T. pulled out the 38 from his waist.

"What the fuck?", Frenchy yelled, startled. "What's goin on?", he added.

"Sit the fuck down", S.T. yelled. Frenchy did as he was

told.

"What's goin on Mookie", Frenchy now asked.

Mookie sat down on the couch.

"Bobby ain't been in charge for a while, Daniel's running things now."

"Martin's Boy?"

"Yeah, and he's been looking all over for you, because you robbed Tony on 143rd, that was Daniel's shit you took."

"Man fuck Danny, that boy don't know how me and his daddy got down, he better ask. Put that fuckin gun away, I practically help raise that boy. He better, show me some fuckin love."

S.T. was shocked at how disrespectful this crack head's mouth was, it didn't matter, Danger and Ad would be back in a moment.

"So you workin for Danny Warren now huh, not an ounce of loyalty in you, bitch." (Slap) S.T. smacked him with the pistol. Frenchy fell to the floor.

"Don't you ever disrespect her."

"Aggghhh", Frenchy groaned in pain as blood from his eye ran down his cheek.

Now Frenchy began to laugh,

"I see…you got another young nigga fooled."

"And what does that mean?", Mookie asked.

"They still don't know who you are?"

Just then the door knocked, still Frenchy laughed, S.T. opened the door. Danger walked in, "Fuckin Frenchy."

Now Frenchy's laughing stopped, Danger followed Adrian, when Frenchy saw Adrian he was stunned.

"Adrian", Frenchy called out.

"Ad you know this asshole?"

"Yeah, I know him."

"You know me.", Frenchy interrupted. "You know me, that's all you have to say"

"Shut the fuck up Frenchy, you cock sucking thief motherfucker", Danger said, pulling out his forty-five.

"How do you know him Ad?", S.T. now asked. Adrian shook his head.

"Where's your heart boy?", Frenchy asked.

"Shut the fuck up Frenchy", Danger once again yelled.

"What's goin on?", Danger added.

"Frenchy's his father", Mookie finally answered.

"What", S.T. said.

"You heard her, I'm his father and you know who she is right?"

"Just shut the fuck up Frenchy", Adrian said.

Everyone was quiet except Frenchy who continued to giggle.

"Frenchy, shut the fuck up", Danger said putting down his 45.

"Is it true A?"

Now Adrian nodded.

"Yeah, he's my father."

"Yeah, Daniel I'm his fuckin father, now untie my fuckin hands." Danger signaled to S.T. to untie Frenchy.

"Wait", Adrian said grabbing S.T.'s shoulder.

"He's my father but that don't change the fact that he's a motherfuckin thief."

"What...what you talkin bout Adrian?", Frenchy said.

Adrian looked at him.

"Shut the fuck up Frenchy, you killed my mother. Ya'll all the family I got, I don't give a fuck about this mother fucker", he said pointing to Frenchy.

"This motherfucker ain't never did shit for me. I wouldn't spit on this motherfucker if he was on fire." S.T. laughed.

"I might use that in a rhyme."

"I ain't jokin Shawn." Nobody called him Shawn, so they knew Adrian was serious now.

Adrian took the fifth out of Dangers hand.

"Right now it's about Harlem. It's about us, this is a family, something some of us know nothing about but I'd die for ya'll niggas. I am my brother's keeper and ain't shit coming between us." (Bang) Frenchy's chair flung backwards as blood slowly accumulated under Frenchy's lifeless body. Adrian had killed his own father. Mookie just stood there, both hands covering her mouth; she couldn't believe what she had just seen. Now they had a body to get rid of.

"Dammit", Mookie screamed.

"You better fix my locks Danger."

S.T. and Danger couldn't help but to laugh, they thought she was going to say something about the body lying on her living room floor, but instead she's talking about the locks. Adrian handed Danger the 45 and walked out the door, Danger limped after him down the hallway. It was hard to understand what Adrian was going through, he just killed his father. Danger tried to relate but he could barely picture Showtime's face.

"A, Yo A wait." Adrian stopped.

"Dog, you alright?"

"No man, how the fuck could I possibly be alright, I just killed my father. I'm fucked up right now."

"You said it, we family now, we all we got, we're brothers, what's mine is yours."

"And what's mine is yours", Adrian added.

"I know it hurt you, but you might have ended his misery."

"Yeah, that's why I did it."

"Now go clean this shit up, dammit, I'm still in pain, got me out of bed, ya'll could've handled this without me."

Decons was slowly dying out, with S.T.'s success, Danger had damn near disowned L.P. and King James, but still the Rappers mentioned both names in their music, Danger and King James. Budda Bless had a single in heavy rotation 'I'll Finish You Cats', one part of the song referenced

"shit Dangerous saved ya life cause I'm the type to
permanently put out your lights, next time a lame touch my
chain I'll take him and blow out his brain I'm talkin to a
Bitch Nigga named King James."

This had James steaming, they rode all through Brooklyn
looking for Budda but he was on tour promoting the new
album, so they approached the closest thing to him D-Most.

"I want this nigga dead Most", James yelled.

"Don't you think you're over reacting",

D-Most took a deep breath, he knew what they wanted.

"Alright, how much?"

"20 gees", L.P. said,

Most rested his head in his hand; he rubbed his eyes with
his thumb and index finger.

"Alright", D-Most agreed,

That had been way too easy for James, so greed took over.

"Nah, Nah, I want 60, yeah sixty gees."

"What, you gotta be kiddin me",

D-Most said looking at L.P, who himself couldn't believe
James thirst.

"I ain't got sixty gees."

"Come on, Budda sold 650 thousand on his last album"

"Alright, listen, I'll set up a nice little hit, Budda's got close to 90 gees worth of jewelry, will beat at Pops Crib Friday night."

Pops Crib was one of the hottest studios in Manhattan.

"L.P., no guns."

"How we gonna do a robbery with no guns", James asked.

"Alright, no shootin, agreed."

Both men shook their heads, so they discussed the details, it would be a smooth robbery. D-Most had an insurance policy on Budda's jewels, so no one would lose.

"L.P., King James", they stopped, turned around and looked at D-Most

"we know, no shooting."

"Yo Danger."

"What up dog",

Adrian and Danger were always together after Adrian killed Frenchy. Danger almost felt obligated to be by his side.

"Danny"

"Oh shit, what's the deal, you callin me by government, what's wrong"

Danger could see how depressed Adrian was, his first child was due any minute, he had a lot on his plate at once besides Jessica, Alexis still nagged him, he was now paying both their rents. "You ever think about going to see your pops?"

"Come on man, for what, what could he possibly say to me."

"That's not the point Danger."

"That is the fuckin point he fucked up my life and my mothers, that nigga ain't never comin home and if he was home he'd be better off fuckin dead."

"I'm sayin."

"That's it A, leave it alone."

"But."

"That's it."

They drove the rest of the way in silence; Adrian had over 75 thousand in the trunk. They walked into the barbershop, everyone greeted them. As usual, Benny Yayo was in the back office. They walked in. Benny was the first person they knew to have all the latest technology. He sat behind his desk playing with his Apple computer, the shit was huge, took up damn near the entire desk.

"Ah Ad, Danger, mi hermanos, que paso?"

"Ain't nothing",

Adrian said tossing the Jansport knapsack to Benny. By now, they were so tight; Benny didn't even bother counting their money anymore.

"So Benny, with that computer, can you find out where someone is in prison", Adrian asked. "Yeah, you have a name."

"Martin Warren." Danger sucked his teeth.

"You just can't leave that shit alone." Benny typed the name into the computer.

"Otisville Federal Pen, here, you need an address?"

"Send Bradshaw into my office right away."

"Yes Senator",

The secretary quickly paged William. William called the secretary back and told her he was busy in turn.

"Senator, Bradshaw says he's busy." Bakemen fumbled with the intercom.

"Tell Bradshaw to get his fucking ass in my office ASAP", his yelling could be heard throughout the office. In minutes Bradshaw walked into Bakemen's office.

"You wanted to see me Harper?"

"Just what the fuck are you doing?" Bakemen now stood up.

"I tell you to go after Junior Carposi and you're busy trying to make deals with Stagalini."

William was shocked, he had no idea how Bakemen could have gotten this information.

"I thought it would help my case against Junior"

"Who the fuck pays you to think, you don't do what you think you should do, you do what I tell you…sit the fuck down."

William had no choice but to do as Bakemen said.

"William don't act like you don't know what's going on."

"Bakemen, I'm on your side, I just want to put these guys away for good."

Bakemen watched William with his hands folded under his chin.

"Cut the bullshit William, you fuck with me, I fuck with you",

Bakemen slid two files across the table, the first read Phillip Bradshaw. It was his parole board review paper stamped denied. The second file read Monica Bradshaw. William could only shake his head no, in disbelief as he read several gees jury indictments.

"You see William, for years these indictments have just disappeared, but now I see I have to threaten those around me because violence is the only thing that warrants respect, so be prepared to have one of your ADA's try a few of these indictments."

Bradshaw grabbed the files, stood up; he wanted badly to say something but the smug smile on Bakemen's face disgusted him. William turned to walk out.

"William." William turned to face the Senator.

"Be careful, this is a do and die business."

"You know what Senator…your right, violence is all some men respect",

William continued out of Bakemen's office. What the fuck was he gonna do, he had Stagalini ready to testify on Bakemen, Junior and Jimmy Carposi, but now the entire plan had to be reevaluated. There would be a lot of consequences involved here. One thing for sure, it was time to check out the old neighborhood.

It is what it Is

Adrian drove; it would be a 7-hour ride, except for DFY. Danger had never been upstate New York, he had no idea you could drive seven hours and still be in New York. His heart pounded, it was his nerves bothering him. He couldn't even remember what his father looked like. The ride was silent; neither knew what to say to the other. So they just drove pass farms Danger saw a part of New York he refused to see when he was a child in DFY. Now he paid attention to the rivers and the mountains. Shit, New York was actually beautiful outside the projects, maybe this could be a life for him, and he smiled to himself. Then once again his mind drifted to thoughts of what Adrian was going through, what was to say Danger wouldn't' feel the same way Adrian had. Plenty of nights Danger had wished he could kill Showtime, now in a few hours he'd be face to face with him.

Adrian on the other hand wasn't thinking about Frenchy, Danger or Showtime. His thoughts at the moment were selfish, he couldn't help but wonder if he was making the right decision, nah he was the biggest asshole. How the fuck could he have chosen Harlem dope blocks over the NFL million dollar contracts for thousand dollar bricks. Yes, it was no doubt about it, he was a stupid motherfucker. He had damn near tossed Alexis to the curb for Jessica, whose only concern was her hair and nails, but this was what he had chosen, this was the life he wanted the excitement, the thrill he had traded his childhood dream for dope dealing nightmares and also his first love for a fat ass and a smile. Then he wondered what could Danger be thinking, he was about to see his pops. The last time he saw Showtime, Danger was ten, now he was 26.

"It's after 1 am and we're an hour away", Adrian said.

"Let's stop at a motel", Danger replied.

It was one fifteen in the morning when the Lexus pulled up at 318 W 32nd and 12th Ave, Pops Crib Studios. It was a big deal tonight, Budda Bless on a collaboration with the Face Man out of Texas; this would be the hottest joint on the street. Budda parked the Lexus GS 400 and finished his bottle of Hennessey and the half of Philly blunt in the ashtray. He was ready to outshine this West Coast cat, this was gonna be the album to crush the East Coast West Coast beef, that's why Budda agreed to do it, he also knew this would boost his West Coast buzz. Budda popped in the cassette that D-Most gave him with the beat they'd be using, he listened as he rolled up some more weed.

"New York is mine I'm hot like a crooked cop wit a loaded nine I'm the Beast in the East while Face is the best in the west cat jealous so I stay with the vest."

He had finished rolling weed, placed the blunt behind his ear. He stepped out the car, just then two masked gunmen approached from behind.

"Budda run it",

The first one said, Budda turned around to stare down the barrel of the three eighty.

"What the fuck is this?"

"Take all that shit off", the second one yelled.

"No ya'll gonna have to kill me, nigga I'm from Brooklyn, Budda said with pride. "Motherfucker give me this motherfuckin chain"

The second man snatched it, Budda snatched off his mask.

"King James", Budda said in shock.

"Yeah that's right, I want all that shit" Now L.P. took off his mask, the jig was up.

"I thought niggas wanted peace?", Budda pleaded.

"Oh, this ain't got shit to do with S.T. or Danger. Now take off the watch and the rings."

"No fuck you", Budda said.

"What", King James yelled, Budda slowly reached behind his back.

Then (Bang), (Bang), (Bang), King hit him three times,

Budda fell backwards, blood splashing on his Lexus.

"King, D said no shooting", L.P. yelled.

"Fuck that nigga and fuck this nigga, just get the jewelry."

L.P. did as he was told as Budda moaned and groaned in pain, they got all the jewels. Budda had his hand on the Desert Eagle; he slowly pulled it from behind his back.

"You heard me Budda fuck you." (Bang)(Bang)(Bang)

"Let's get the fuck out of here",

L.P. said as the two ran down the street, guns and jewels in hand. They had left Budda there to die, it was after 1:30 am, Budda's car phone was ringing as he lay in his own blood on the concrete he dug in his pocket finding his lighter he lit the blunt that was behind his ear, a pedestrian screamed,

"Oh my God, call an ambulance."

Budda made it to his feet; he stumbled into the corridor of Pops Cribs still smoking his weed. It was late, the front doors were opened but there was no security, something was wrong. He made his way to the elevator and pushes the button. The woman from outside ran in behind him.

"Sir the police and ambulance are on the way."

"Tha...thank...you", he said falling to the ground. The elevator doors opened; there was D-Most, Face, and Cash Rock.

"Oh shit, it's Budda", Face yelled.

"What happened my nigga", he added.

"He got shot."

D-Most dropped by his side to see if he was still conscious, although he was completely quiet, he was still breathing. Thank God it was midtown. It only took the ambulance 25 minutes to arrive. They rushed the unconscious Budda Bless to Bellevue Medical Center in Manhattan.

It was a little after 8 am, when Adrian walked past the morning newspaper in the motel lobby. He paid no attention to it or its headline

'Thug Rapper Plugged'

It was the media's poor attempt to take a stab at hip-hop. The front page read 'Gangster Thug Rapper Budda Bless was gunned down late last night on his way to record with Texas gangster Rapper Face Man. Sources say this could be retaliation for West Coast Rapper Murder Jay getting jumped at the Video Awards in February. Bellevue release the statement that Budda Bless whose real name is Bernard Bless, is in stable condition after being shot six times including one shot that just grazed his head, just like his hit song a year ago 'It Not Your Time', it wasn't't his.'

"You ready?", Adrian asked.

"As ready as I could possibly be",

Danger replied as they walked in the direction of the Federal Penitentiary. It was disgusting what they put visitors through. They literally treat visitors like prisoners, just to see their family. Searches were degrading to both parties, prisoners, and their families. Adrian and Danger finally made it through what seemed like post 9-11 airport security. Police sat them at a table near the officer's desk.

"Excuse me officer, can we get a different table?", asked Adrian.

"No", the officer barked.

"Man fuck him, let's just sit down", Danger said, his heart pounding, he had never in his life been so nervous, he wanted to leave but after going through so much to get in there it made no sense to leave, it was time to see his dad.

When Showtime walked in, it was easy to see he was Danger's dad, they looked just alike. Showtime's build was amazing for his age, but they say prison preserves a man youth and he had been locked up sixteen years already. Showtime walked right over to the table, he extended his hand, and both Danger and Adrian stood up.

"Damn Daniel, you have your mother's eyes", he said shaking his hand.

Danger sat back down.

"And who are you", Showtime asked Adrian.

"Adrian Walker sir", Adrian answered, now shaking his hand.

"Oh, you Frenchy's boy, sorry to hear what happened to him." They both looked at him shocked.

"Don't be surprised; shit in here, we hear about what goes on before half the hood knows."

He looked at both of them.

"What ya'll niggas scared?", he asked.

"A little, Mr. Showtime", Adrian answered.

"Don't worry, I ain't gonna bite you and please don't call me Showtime, that man was dead a long time ago, so Daniel I hear you the man in Harlem." Danger said nothing.

"Yep, we control damn near everything from 116th to 145, but it's only like five spots", Adrian answered.

"I also hear you into this music thing." Still Danger said nothing.

"I-ACOCA Records, Danger built the entire thing by himself, we just opened a small office in Mid Town."

Martin just stared at his son.

"Daniel, Daniel I'm sorry. I never meant to leave you or your mother, I knew if I hadn't gone to prison Viv would still be here, you look so much like her." For the first time

Danger spoke.

"I always hear how much I look like you." Martin smiled.

"That's all you got to say to your dad?"

"What do you want me to say Showtime?"

"Wait, don't call me Showtime, I'm your father."

"Well it's hard to tell."

"Look, maybe you ain't ready for this, maybe you should come back when you've grown up a little."

"Grown up a little, Martin I'm a man, I take care of my responsibilities unlike you."

"And what the fuck does that mean?"

"Come on Martin, you left us with nothing."

Martin couldn't believe what he was hearing; he leaned back in his chair and folded his arms. "That's why Vivian's not here, she had to prostitute to give me the little bit she could."

A tear ran down Danger's cheek.

"While you had it easy, we suffered in the street poor."

"You finished", Martin asked.

"Yeah, I'm finished, Adrian let's get the fuck outta here."

Both of them stood up as if ready to leave, Martin jumped

to his feet, the guards quickly rushed over.

"Everything's cool", Martin assured the guard.

"Are you sure", the guard asked Danger and Adrian, Adrian nodded yes.

"Sit down Daniel." Adrian sat down.

"Sit Down Daniel." Martin said in a more authoritative voice and Danger did as his father said. "First off, do you think this shit has been easy, you did six years so you tell me do you think this shit has been easy", Martin said raising his voice,

, Danger shook his head.

"Anyone in Harlem could tell you how I loved your mother and you from the day you were born. You were treated like a prince, you never wanted for anything, your mother, your mother", Martin was choked up as if trying to fight back tears.

"She was everything to me."

"What about the drugs dad?"

"What could I do Daniel, I couldn't' count the mornings I sat up with her as she tried to kick the sickness, but I couldn't stand to see her in that pain"

Both Martin and Danger were crying now.

"So why didn't you leave her with anything?"

"Daniel I left everything."

"Dammit we had nothing."

"That's impossible; I left Bobby with over twenty million, shit I left too much to count."

"He gave me nothing."

That was how the end started after all these years. Danger found out his dad hadn't shitted on him and his mom. They talked about the night Martin was arrested, there was only three people that knew where he was headed, Martin, Bobby and Josephine who was in the car with Martin the day he lost his life. It had to be Bobby after seventeen years. It made sense. The tension was gone; the rest of the visit was peaceful, smiles and laughs. It ended with hugs and promises of keeping in touch which was kept.

"Do me a favor son, find Josephine, I want to see her. She also has money of mine; Mookie should be able to find her."

That was if Danger would be back, twice that month but the next visit he had business to take care of.

"My Dad wasn't, an asshole."

"Yeah, just think you didn't want to come."

"Word, thanks A."

"C'mon that's what brothers are for, but you know what we gotta do right."

"Way ahead of you."

They rode back to New York City. Danger thought about how police made them sit up front, scared Martin would give away some kind of info. In seventeen years, so many reporters had visited him looking for his story. Martin 'Showtime' Warren was a prison celebrity and prisoner celebrities were a threat to the system because everyone wants to hear what they have to say.

"Why would you even come down here?", Mookie asked.

"I needed to talk to you", her brother answered.

"Wow, after ten years you've remember the po people in da ghetto, sir", she said sarcastically. "We're on opposite sides of the track, you do what you do and I do what I do but I've never stopped loving you."

"So what do you want", she said trying hard to relax, she just felt so uncomfortable.

"Dammit, you could have had me meet you somewhere else", she added.

"I can leave if you want me to", he said not really meaning his words,

then there was the knock at the door. It was Sunday afternoon, so they weren't worried about police but still her heart pounded.

"Oh my God, you're gonna get me killed."

"Just answer the door Mookie." Mookie could barely
breathe if anyone was to see him here. She was a dead
woman. She shook her head as she walked to the door,
whoever it was still knocked.

"Who is it?"

"S.T."

"What the fuck is this",

Danger said as they pulled up to his Park Avenue
Brownstone which was surrounded by cops. "Get the fuck
outta here Adrian."

Adrian wasted no time pealing out. Danger and Ad still
had no idea about the Friday night shooting; Danger dialed
S.T. on the cell phone.

"Yo, damn dog, where you been", S.T. answered.

"What's goin on?", Danger asked.

"Not on the phone Dee, but we gotta talk."

"Where are you?"

"Mookie's but come clean, we got company." S.T. hung up,

Danger didn't know what to make of anything, but jail wasn't an option. Adrian kept looking into the rearview mirror.

"Why do you keep doin that?"

"I don't know if I'm buggin or what but I swear there's a beige fifth avenue following us, don't look back, just chill", Adrian said as he made the left turn.

"Is it still there", Danger asked.

"Hold on…yeah", Adrian answered.

Without signaling, Adrian jumped into the right lane, the 5th Avenue slowly made its way into the right lane.

"You think it's police?"

"Nah, I don't think so." Adrian sped up; he was doing almost sixty down St. Nick.

"Whoa, slow down",

Danger said as Adrian swerved through the traffic, he made it to Mookie's block, he was certain that they weren't the police now. Both men quickly jumped out the car and hurried into the building. They realized two things the men weren't police but they were definitely following them. They ran up the stairs to the fourth floor, Danger pounded on the door, he couldn't help but think it was as hit and neither of them had a weapon.

"Who is it", Danger heard Mookie ask.

"It's me Ma, open the door."

Mookie opened the door without looking, inside the apartment A and Danger jumped in and poked their heads out and watched the hallway.

"What's wrong with ya'll", S.T. asks

"Sssh",

Adrian said without looking back waving his hand at S.T., no one had followed them upstairs. Adrian turned first, Danger locked the door then turned around his heart dropped, his mouth instantly dried he couldn't swallow he couldn't believe who was sitting in Mookie's living room. "Monica, is this him?",

the man said standing up extending his hand.

"Yes", Mookie answered.

"Daniel Warren."

Danger thought he was being set up he couldn't believe it of all people to set him up S.T. and Mookie.

"Yes, Daniel meet my brother", Mookie said,

"William Bradshaw.

THE BEGINNING

"Yes, boss it's the same address, I don't know if they went into the same apartment but I'm looking at Bradshaw's wife's car."

"What the fuck is going on, you listen to me I don't care if you gotta sit out there till next Thursday as soon as Bradshaw and Warren leave you call me, it's time to play hard ball now", Bakemen hung up. He knew who lived in the tenement he also knew what his next move would be but was it possible that Bradshaw himself had his hand in the cookie jar. Quickly he dialed another number after three rings it was answered.

"Yo", the other line picked up (click, click).

"It's me say no names."

"Why are you so paranoid?"

"Because the phone lines are never safe."

"Yeah well what can I do you for?"

"The Banker."

"Done, also the nigger uptown and the dummy spic, I've got my boys on him right now."

(click, click)

"What was that?", he asked nervously

. "What was what", the other line asked.

"Did you hear a clicking where are you?", he asked. "Home, where else?"

"Alright I gotta go I'll give you a call later this week, remember anyone who can tie me to Donahue."

"I know; I know ex em out." Both men hung up.

"Who the hell was that…anyone, somebody tell me something."

Agent Spence was in charge of the investigation; no one could tell him anything.

"Nobody recognizes the voice."

Still everyone sat with blank expressions on their faces.

"Spence we're running the number now I should have a name for you in a few minutes", another Agent told the supervisor.

"Spence he did mention Donahue so it has to be our guy."

"Yes Katts but the question is who's Our Guy."

"I got it", the Agent called out.

"What", asked Spence.

"The number is listed under the name Lisa Morning."

"And who the hell is she", Katts asked.

"Get this", another Agent said smiling.

"Lisa Morning is the secretary of Attorney General William Bradshaw."

"You gotta be fuckin kidding me", Spence said in disbelief.

"Isn't that who took down Jimmy Carposi Sr.", Katts asked.

Spence nodded as he read the print out.

"Do you think Junior Carposi had something to do with his father's arrest?" Katts nodded.

"I don't know, but I want 24-hour surveillance on Bradshaw ASAP."

"Right Boss right away."

"What the fuck is going on here, we have the mob, Attorney Generals, street thugs and a police commissioner."

"Spence, Carposi's on the move."

"Get a man on him."

"Done."


S.T. explained the shooting of Budda Bless, Budda lived and told police it was L.P. and King James. Now not only were they on the run but they had incriminated I-ACOCA Records. For some reason it was said that Danger orchestrated the entire robbery and attempted murder. "Bradshaw you've got to help me I didn't even know what was going on, L.P. and James aren't even on my team."

"I understand and I'll do what I can but what you need to worry about is the fact that Bakemen wants you dead."

"What?"

"Yeah Adrian the night Fame Anderson was murdered it was a hit called by Junior Carposi and Harper Bakemen."

"If you know this why don't you do something about it William"

"Monica were talking about a United States Senator not a street hustler."

"Don't you guys have Internal Affairs", Danger asked.

"Or maybe call in the Feds", Adrian added.

"Listen it's not that simple somehow Bakemen knows my every move. I have Reggie Stagalini." "Carposi's hit man I know em", Danger said.

William nodded his head as he tossed the folder on the table. Mookie picked it up Danger watch along over her shoulder.

"When Bakemen heard I had Stagalini ready to testify I received that."

It was Phillips parole denial and Mookie's indictments.

"How is this possible", Mookie said.

"I don't know but I need you guys. I'm working on a plan I don't know what it is yet but I need you guys to stay off the radar no drugs nothing."

"Damn Bradshaw, I got five keys that have to be paid for", Adrian said.

"You can't do anything were all being followed shit they might know we're all together now both of you know someone was following you but we don't know who. Nothing, don't even sell oil or incense on 125th if you want us all to walk away from this trust me."

So just like that they were to turn off all business. Danger decided the best thing to do was explain to Benny what was going on and give back the coke. So he, S.T. and Adrian would take a ride uptown.

They jumped in S.T.'s, ride constantly checking the rearview but it didn't seem like anyone was following them so they sped off. William walked out the door skeptical he looked each way intensively he knew without a doubt he was being followed, he smiled for all viewers there was actually two cars following him one snapped his photo. William climbed into his Lincoln Continental he sat there for a moment adjusting his mirrors,

"How the fuck did I get myself into this shit",

He wondered but he wasn't gonna run. No he was gonna stay and fight, it wouldn't be easy to get rid of him. What Bakemen and the others forgot was William was from the street he still could play as dirty if not dirtier. William pulled off watching his rearview. A few seconds later a crown Victoria slowly pull off behind him.

"Boss Bradshaw's leaving."

"Get rid of her, and nothing rough just how I told you."

"Got it."

Two men got out of the 5th Avenue they walked into the building climbing the stairs to the fourth floor. They knocked on the door.

"Who is it", Mookie asked.

"NYPD", a voice answered.

"Shit", Mookie whispered.

"Give me one minute",

She replied, as she looked around S.T. and Adrian had collected everything so she doubted there were any drugs. The door knocked again,

"I'm coming",

Mookie called out, she took a deep breath and was now opening the door.

"I'm sorry it took so long I wasn't dressed, how can I help you officer?"

(Slap) One of the men hit her sending her small fragile body crashing into the table, the same man quickly rushed her kicking her in the stomach, causing her to spit blood.

"Beckett", Lipsett called out,

"that's enough, let's do what we came to do."


Benny understood but what he was afraid of was if anyone followed them to his place.

"Danger if you're being fuckin watched why would you come here."

Danger couldn't say anything Benny was right. What was worse is Danger couldn't even tell Benny who was watching them but at that exact moment Benny wanted to kill Danger and his crew.

"Its stupid mistakes like this Danger that put men in prison for a long time."

"I apologize Benny."

"Yeah just get the fuck out of my shop."

Danger, S.T. and Adrian walked out Benny picked up his phone it rang twice,

"Yeah."

"Junior its Benny…… you still wanna deal?"

With Danger and Adrian scared of the game Benny needed someone who could move almost as much coke as the Harlem boys.

"So what happen to make you change your mind Benny the Moolie's from uptown find a new connect?"

"No it's just that I have something big coming in."

"I see maybe we could work out something better."

Junior Carposi saw his opportunity. He knew if Benny was calling him for something, something had to go wrong with them Harlem Niggers. The funny thing was if there was one thing Carposi hated it was niggers and, the only thing he hated more than niggers was a spic.

"So what are you talkin Junior?"

"Well I know you're charging 15 for the key."

"17"

"Well, I have a warehouse right next to the airport."

"Queens."

"More like Long Island."

"So", Benny said.

"So at 13 you could also have storage"

"14 and you and I can do business."

"Deal."

Danger had been quiet the entire ride to Josephine's. Not only was she still around but she was right in the Bronx. Mookie had the address and everything.

"What's on your mind",

Adrian asked watching the road and the rearview wondering if they were still being followed.

"I don't know for some reason I don't trust Benny."

"What we been fuckin with Benny for a minute", S.T. added.

"Yeah it's different when you bring a man 50 gees a week."

"I know what you mean", Adrian added.

"Maybe we should throw him something to keep him happy"

Adrian had a good idea but it might not have been enough money mad men behave in funny ways besides, Danger knew he already had too many people to kill. Starting with Bobby.

Adrian and Danger walked to the door and rang the bell.

"Just a minute", a sweet sounding voice nearly sung.

It was a nice house in the Throgs Neck Section of the Bronx.

"Who is it?"

"Excuse me ma'am my name is Daniel Warren I came by to deliver",

Before he could finish the door had flown open and he was staring at one of the most beautiful older women he had ever seen.

"Oh my God", she said covering her month,

"Danny."

"Yes", Danger said nodding his head.

"Please come in", they followed her inside.

"Please have a seat, would you like something to drink", she offered, both men nodded.

She left them to go into the kitchen, Danger couldn't help but look around her living room she had lovely taste, Danger got up to look at the pictures she had on her mantle.

"Those were better days", she said.

"Oh excuse me", Danger replied.

"No, no quite alright besides a few of them are you", she said.

Josephine had so much to tell Danger that she really didn't know where to begin. One things for sure she needs him to know, his mother was addict to heroin before she met his father but it was Josephine that took care of an infant Daniel. Vivian was too busy running the streets getting high to take care of a child.

"Your mother was a beautiful woman it was the heroin, it had taken over her, and it was killing your father, he would sit up nights just crying he really didn't know what to do. He would put her in rehabs she'd run away. She honestly didn't want to be helped and it was fucked up. Your dad had so much money and was scared something was gonna happen to him."

"Why was he scared", Adrian asked, Josephine sipped her tea.

"Martin was a good and loyal man at times a little too loyal, if he considered you a friend you were safe you'd never have to worry again", she said waving her hands as if to gesture to the house.

"Ray was jealous."

"Who", Danger asked.

"You look so much like your dad it's amazing, but Bobby Rich, he was Martin's right hand man, but he wanted everything Martin had including your mother, now your mother addiction had gotten so bad, she had a least a five hundred dollar a day habit. Now that's nothing but back then that was damn near 2 grams a day your father would supply it to keep her off the streets, but he couldn't see her so he would send Bobby, and Bobby was such a fuckin snake he would give her half then use the other half to get what he wanted."

"So my mom's was sleeping with Bobby."

"No her addiction was, Bobby would always tell her he loved her and they should be together but your mom loved Martin. When she said to him what about Martin if you could only see the look in Bobby's eyes. It was his love for your mother that put Martin in jail."

"I don't understand", Danger said.

"Bobby wanted your mother, so he set your dad up."

Danger couldn't understand why his father didn't tell him this not only had Bobby deprived Danger's childhood but Bobby was also the reason his dad had to spend his life in prison. A tear ran down Dangers cheek Josephine walked over and wiped it away.

"Enough tears have been shed."

"Does my dad know?"

"Of course, we all knew! That's the only reason your dad had the gun, at the time the late Commissioner Donahue was the partner of the cop your dad killed he called and told me and I told your father."

Danger was letting it all soak in and there was a question burning in his head he wanted desperately to ask but the answer scared him. He wasn't sure he could handle it but Jo must have read his mind.

"Ask, I know you want to and I can't lie. I believe it's why your father sent you to me, he's always been sensitive to the facts of your mother's death, but you have to promise me you will not get caught. We all want the revenge but we couldn't deal with you going to prison for it."

"I don't understand."

"Just promise me you'll be smart."

"Of course."

"With your father gone Vivian was free but her addiction was still major, your dad left everything to you well over 25 million."

Danger felt his heart skip a beat.

Bobby expected Vivian to be his woman. We were all at a party in Manhattan, even for a dope fiend Vivian was beautiful! She hid her train tracks well. Anyway this asshole turns off the music grabs the microphone and proposed to Vivian; Vivian couldn't believe it she just busted out laughing and said 'It's bad enough that I fuck the help for a hit but does this pussy motherfucker think he can afford me.' The entire party laughed at him, she had humiliated him after a few drinks and snorts. It was as if Vivian forgot she had embarrassed him in front of everyone, she told me she was going to get a fix from him I begged her not to go but once she got going you couldn't't stop her, the two of them went outside."

King James felt they had waited long enough it was time to sell Budda's Jewels. They pulled up to Jew Man, a grimy see no evil hear no evil type of man, James had dealt with him in the past and he knew Jew Man wouldn't care about insurance. He had brought Jew Man Jewels with blood still on them. He examined each piece carefully as L.P. and James waited patiently.

"Ah Okay", he said pulling out his calculator punching numbers quickly.

"60 thousand."

"Come on that's over 100 worth of Jewelry."

"Yes but the diamonds are flawed; I'm giving you sixty because I like you." James and L.P. debated for a moment.

"65."

"Agreed."

Jew Man went in the back to his safe never taking his eyes off the monitor. He returned with the 65 gees.

"Jew Man if anyone asks."

"I know I know I got them from a crack head."

L.P. and James got into L.P.'s Benz as James counted out the money.

"You take 35 and I'll take 30", L.P. volunteered.

James said nothing as they headed for the Brooklyn Bridge. Once again the devil was at work as the wheels turned inside James head he wasn't happy with 65 gees he was even less enthusiastic about having to split it.

"Yo pull over I gotta piss", James said.

"Damn you can't wait till we hit BK?"

"Nah nigga it's an emergency pull over on one of them side streets."

L.P. pulled off of Houston Street there was a small lot. James hopped out to take a piss. Loading the 45., he thought about what he was about to do and 65 gees was a descent amount of money but not enough to share. He could shoot this nigga and leave him right here.

"Dammit" he thought to himself. Why the fuck didn't he make sure Budda Bless was dead, because of this niggas carelessness his name was all over the paper, shit that's why he need all this money, he needed it to get out of dodge because he was too hot to stay in New York. He opened the door and got in.

"What the fuck, what the fuck are you doin",

(Bang Bang)

Two shots to the head, that's one thing he never thought about. Now there was blood splattered all over the car.

"Shit",

L.P said as he opened the door and began to drag the bloody body out; he couldn't help but suck his teeth because of all the blood. Even his clothes were covered in blood. He pulled the lifeless body behind the same dumpster he had pissed behind then dug through the pockets.

"Damn James you were my boy but I know you, you were probably thinking the same thing."

L.P. carefully searched James but found no gun. Maybe he was wrong maybe James wasn't plotting but it was too late to dwell on that James was dead. L.P. took off his bloodied shirt and began to wipe down the cars windows he would stop at a car wash and thoroughly clean it after he picked up his shit with the 65 gees he now had well over 100 gees he was out, Fuck New York.

"Who lives here", S.T. asked as they pulled up to the Manhattan address.

"The man who ruined my life", Danger answered.

"So what we gonna do we don't have no guns", Adrian asked.

"I got a can of mace", S.T. added.

"Oh fuckin great were gonna get the man with pepper spray", Adrian laughed.

165 | P a g e

"It's not a joke, but were straight. If we walk up in there, there's no way Bobby's gonna think we don't have guns so wait here."

Danger hoped he was right, one thing he knew for sure Bobby was scared to death of any pressure. The only real worry of Dangers was, getting past the front desk.

"Yes how can I help you", the security guard asked.

"Ray Roberts."

"Ah, and who are you?"

"His son."

The door man gave a funny look as he picked up the phone to call up to Bobby's apartment.

"Yes Mr. Roberts you have a guest; I know sir but he says he's, your son"

The "What", could be heard by Danger,

"Yes, Your son."

Next the guard described Danger.

"I'll send him up."

Danger had done it he was tempted to call S.T. and A but decided to go up himself.

"Apartment 5C."

Danger walked to the elevator, his heart pounding not knowing what his next move was. On the ride up he kept shifting his pager trying to make it look like a gun on his hip the doors opened. Danger stepped out. He walked around the corner right into the barrel of the gun.

"Nigga what the hell are you doin here", Bobby asked putting the gun away.

"I needed to talk to you, man I know you seen the news."

It was quick thinking on Danger's behalf, shit he would have never thought Bobby would get the drop on anyone.

"So what you need to talk about?" Danger sat down.

"What happened with you and my father?"

"C'mon blood that's what you come down her for", Bobby asked nervously.

"Yeah I've heard a lot of fucked up shit lately and everything leads to you."

Bobby sat up and looked at the gun on the table, Danger shook his head and tapped his pager, and Bobby now sat back.

"Who you been listening to man I gave you everything and still you turned around and shitted on me but I never once did anything."

"Bobby you couldn't do anything, who the fuck do you have on your side, who the Carposi's the police"

"Ha come on man what you talkin bout"

"Now what happened with you and my father and before you start, I visited him and he told me his side so be careful."

"I loved your father man, he just didn't understand Harlem was changing and dope was fuckin everything up."

"Including my mother." A tear ran down Bobby's check,

"especially your mother I loved her, he didn't appreciate her and he didn't deserve her."

"And you deserve her?"

"Daniel all your father did was feed her dope he didn't love her like I loved her."

Danger couldn't believe what he was hearing he looked at the gun on the table himself but it wasn't the time or the place.

"So you turned on my pops because you loved my mom's?"

"Hahaha", Bobby laughed nervously.

"What would make you think some bullshit like that, man that's crazy."

"Is it Bobby, who knew my pops was leaving or what car he was in besides you and Josephine?" When Danger mentioned Josephine bobby's aura changed.

"You loved my mom's so much you ratted him out and you killed my mother."

"No Daniel, No Daniel I didn't mean to kill her."

Bobby broke down as he told his side of the story how she screamed and screamed for the dope but he begged her to leave it alone. How he promised to take her out of the Ghetto if only she got help finally she attacked him when he said no.

"I loved her Daniel you gotta believe me I would never have hurt her, you gotta believe me." "You loved her you loved my father what about me what misery besides taking everything my father left me, what other misery have you caused in my life."

Danger now stood up Bobby's hands was literally shaking.

"Nothing I swear Daniel I swear Daniel I got all the money you need man whatever you want." "I don't want nothing from you but you owe me your life remember that."

Danger walked out of the apartment, he stood waiting for the elevator. Bobby stood at his door watching him he couldn't understand why Daniel didn't kill him, he expected to die. The elevator doors opened he got in turning to see Bobby standing there. Before the door closed he mouth the words,

"You owe me your life",

The door closed Danger leaned back against the elevators rear wall and cried he could never even remember the last time he cried. He had shed a tear for Fame when she died but here he was literally bawling in the elevator, the doors opened,

"Get the fuck on the floor get down get fuckin down."

Danger did as he was told, he looked around the cops had S.T. and Adrian all out the car they had torn it apart. None of them had any idea what the cops were looking for but they made sure they searched thoroughly.

"Daniel Warren."

"Yes."

"We're taking you in just for questioning."

"So why such drastic measures, I mean look what you guys did to my man's car",

Danger said as they finally allowed him to get to his feet.

"Well a big pretty brand new car like this, he should have full coverage."

They took Danger to 100 Centre Street they questioned him for hours, but he honestly knew nothing about the robbery he had a better than average alibi. The next questions were all about Lance Palmer which surprised Danger he knew for a fact King James was involved but they said nothing about him.

"Are we done", Danger asked.

"Yeah Warren we're done"

They were done but now the Feds wanted to question him.

"It had to be Danger; I heard L.P. say D said no guns."

"C'mon Budda Danger's a man of his word he wanted peace them niggas was on they own thing. Danger had nothing to do with it."

"Why you defending this nigga",

Budda yelled as D-Most sat in a chair by the hospital room window.

"I ain't defending him I just know L.P. and James are grimy motherfuckers and I don't think Danger had anything to do with it."

"Fuck it, so the Reason is coming to interview me, there talking about giving next month's cover."

Budda was ready to use his misfortune to the best of his ability to boost his image and record sales getting shot was turning out to be one of the best things to happen to him. He had received over 300 phone calls from fans mostly women praying he was alright he also had over 150 guests all brings cards candy and flowers. He picked up the newspaper.

The article read 'Rise of a Soldier: Bernard (Budda) Bless, Rapper to become a victim of his own lyrics. In many songs the controversial rap artist promotes gun violence and street wars but up until now Budda Bless had little in his music to match his perfect life. Bernard grew up in a quiet Canarsie neighborhood in Brooklyn the son of a nurse and a real estate agent.

"Yeah Bernard had everything while we were crying and begging for a pair of Nike Sharks or suede Puma's he had two or three pairs",

An old classmate of his told our reporters we went to his old high school George Washington Carver and spoke to his tenth grade teacher.

"Oh Bernard lovely gentleman very welled manner oh he loved the theater that's why I was surprised when he transferred to the school of the performing arts."

Something that the average thug doesn't do is perform Shakespeare we sat down with his baby's mother, what could you tell us about Budda.

"Bernard is so sweet he's nothing like his music".'

Those were the words that forced Budda to react he had to do something he decided to sign out the hospital five days after being shot six times he wanted out of the hospital. He signed out unable to walk. The doctors cautioned him but he refused to listen, his image was on the line he had a lot of shit to prove he personally felt his career depended on it.

"D-Most get me a gun as soon as possible."

"For what Budda, so you can do something stupid."

"Nah ain't gonna be nothing stupid but niggas are gonna respect me."

Budda was serious he was really going to change his image and until the day of his tragic murder he had lived what he chose to rap about.

Danger had only heard stories about the Feds he had never dealt with them and for the first time he could even recall in his life he was scared.

"So Mister Warren Aka Danger do you know who we are", Agent Spence asked.

"Yeah the Feds", Danger answered. Agent Spence smiled.

"So Danger, can I call you Danger."

Danger shrugged his should as if to say he didn't care.

"Well is there anything you want to tell me."

"I told the police everything I knew which is nothing", once again Spence smiled.

"Let me tell you something I know every motherfucking thing about you from your dope fiend mother to what you had for dinner last night, your left handed, you got a birthmark on your right shoulder and your allergic to strawberries so don't fuck with me now tell me about these."

Spence threw 8 by 10's of Danger with Junior Carposi in Jimmy's a few with Bobby Rich and just today standing outside of Mookie's house followed by a photo of William Bradshaw standing in the same spot.

"Now talk to me Daniel."

"What do you want me to say?"

"You don't seem to understand Daniel your fucked."

Danger knew Spence was bluffing. The feds didn't have shit on him and he knew what he didn't know was what they wanted.

"So what's William Bradshaw into."

"He's the Attorney General what do you mean."

"Dammit", Spence said slamming his hands on the desk.

"What the fuck is going on in Harlem and what do William Bradshaw and Harper Bakemen have to do with it?"

Now Danger understood that's who was watching him the Feds, stupid motherfuckers always on the wrong man, shit Bradshaw wanted to bring Bakemen down and the Feds were lost ready to take down the wrong man.

"Listen ain't shit goin on in Harlem just music. If you know everything about me then you know I ain't in the game no more. I'm a CEO."

"Yeah of I-ACOCA Records, you passed the drug game down to Adrian Walker, what a fuckin waste that boy was a hell of a running back and threw it all away to be a crack dealer. Tell me, is there really that much money in the ghetto? All you motherfucking jungle monkey's driving Beamers and Benz's. Anyways I-ACOCA Records is that the cover up is that what you're telling me."

"No but after all these years we find out Mookie…. is Monica Bradshaw", Danger nodded his head in agreement.

"So who's responsible for this",

Spence ask tossing another photo on the desk in front of Danger. Danger looked at them.

"Oh my God what fuckin time is it?" Danger asked

Spence looked at his watch.

"1600, 19hours."

"What?"

"4:19."

"What time was this picture taken?"

"Two hours after you and your boys left we went to question her."

"Can I use a phone?"

"Yeah but don't run anywhere."

Danger was so discombobulated he could barely dial the number.

"Yeah."

"Adrian its Dee."

"Yeah man you alright?"

"Yeah they just been questioning me all night."

"You still there."

"Yeah listen they, where's S.T.?"

"Down on the couch why what's up?"

"They found Mookie dead."

The picture Spence showed Danger was of a naked overdosed Mookie still with the needle in her arm. By 6 am Spence let Danger go he jumped in a cab to Adrian and Jessica's house. It was early in the morning and Danger didn't want to disturb her, she was due but something needed to be done and if it wasn't the Feds that killed Monica it had to be Bakemen and Carposi. S.T. answered the door in tears. Although everyone knew about their love affair Mookie and S.T. tried to keep it hidden.

"You alright, yeah man scared to call my mom's."

"Why?"

"Dog my mom's has our baby."

That's what no one knew everyone knew Mookie had a baby but no one knew her baby father was S.T.

"Nigga somebody gone die."

Danger couldn't believe how emotional S.T. was, they walked into the living room William Bradshaw sat on the love seat, and he stood when Danger entered.

"William you alright."

"Yeah it's S.T. I'm worried about he told me I have a

niece."

"Yeah God Bless, you making funeral arrangements?"

"Yes so Adrian's telling me about the Feds."

"Yeah they're watching you they asked me a few questions but mostly they want to know about you and Bakemen."

"They have me tied into Bakemen's bullshit."

"Yeah its seems so."

"Maybe that was his plan", Adrian added.

"What do you mean", William asked.

"Bakemen knew shit couldn't last forever and one day he would need someone to take the fall, who better than the nappy head Negro lawyer from Harlem."

"It makes sense; William you were the best candidate. Your families from the hood, your brother was a dope dealer and even your sisters in the game. You look guilty automatically", Danger said.

"If I'm involved or not."

"So what do we do Danger", S.T. asked he only had revenge on his mind.

Danger sat quiet for a moment.

"We do nothing we sit back."

"What?" S.T. yelled.

"S, I promise you Carposi will pay…. right away but that has to be done outside the radar the Feds are watching all of us so we have to move smart and do a little research, we can't just go wild wild west there's too much at stake. Since we're being watched its time for us to start watching everyone else", everyone agreed.

"William business as usual you know nothing about your sister's death you just grieve but make sure Bakemen believes you've taken the message; Ad you get us some good drivers I want at least two cars on Junior Carposi at all times I know he's an easy target, S we're not hustling I need you to focus on your music a few mix tapes can help with the bills you just hold your head we all loved Mookie."

"I can help you with bills too, I'm not crooked but I have made a few dollars on the side anything you guys need just let me know."

It was greatly appreciated everyone knew what they had to do so right away they got started.

"Who is she William?"

"Oh my God do we have to go through this Sandra there is no other woman."

Although his career was finally where Sandra wanted, Williams's business affairs began falling apart and once again his life at home was crumbling.

"I'm sick and tired of it all William, the days of you disappearing as well as the phone calls", William was stuck for a moment.

"Phone calls?"

"Yes William late night phone calls and I know it's a woman, I can hear the little bitch laughing."

"Since when?"

"What does it matter William",

She didn't understand and wouldn't understand if William tried to explain it to her, but for right now William would let the little game play out but now Bakemen was going a little too far fucking with his family.

"I look into our bank book William and there's 10 thousand dollars missing how do you explain that?"

"I have something that needs to be taken care of you wouldn't understand right now."

"William I am your wife and if you can't be honest with me maybe this marriage isn't worth trying to save",

she turned and walked out of the kitchen. Sandra never knew anything about Phillip or Monica. They had been chapters of his life he had tried to erase. And until he met Daniel Warren, William had truly forgotten who he was by ignoring his family. He was hiding who he was. It was time to tell Sandra the truth. He would start with this weekend. Although he was drop dead tired William still put on his suit and drove into Harlem for work.

"Good Morning Lisa."

"Rough night."

"Yeah I didn't get any sleep see if you can set up a meeting with Bakemen for me I need a few days." Daniel went into his office closing the door behind him.

Mrs. Lisa Morning picked up the phone.

"Mr. Bakemen its Lisa."

"Yes Lisa did William make it in this morning?"

"Yes sir he needs to see you; he says he needs a couple of days."

Bakemen found that odd William made his own hours if he needed a few days he could take them on his own.

"Well how does he look?"

"Tired sir."

"Well tell him about ten thirty."

10:30 am William knocked on Bakemen's office door.

"Come in William", he entered with his hands raised in the air. Bakemen smiled,

"What's going on William?"

"You win."

"What",

Bakemen stood up and walked around his desk, he stood face to face with William.

"What are you talking about", Bakemen asked.

"My sister you win I understand".

Bakemen placed his hand on William's chest.

"Yes I've heard about your sister's tragic accident", he said pat frisking William to see if he was wearing a wire.

"I'm not wearing a wire Harper. I can't win I realize this, but please leave my wife alone. I'll do whatever you want, just leave what little family I have left, out of this."

"It's about time you woke up. You could be rich by now; don't you understand the American dream is full of shit. America became successful off the misery of others when they say only the strong survive it is not a quote or a saying it is the American Bible. America can't be saved the plans from the beginning was to suck it dry of all its resources then say fuck it. How do they say in the ghetto roll or get rolled over? Crack is the new gold. I did this to New York, I said fuck heroin it's time for something new. Gold is 7 dollars a gram by next year crack will be damn near 20 to 25 dollars a gram. I am the future and either you'll be a part of it or you'll be past tense." "I'm with you", William answered.

"First I want all your files on Junior Carposi, Donahue and Stagalini ASAP."

"Yes sir I'll get on it right away", William turned to leave.

"Oh Bradshaw", Bakemen called stopping William in his tracks.

"Yes", William answered trying to keep his composure.

"Just in case you have any other bright ideas I've been playing golf on the weekends at a Country Club in Westchester with Jefferson so do be careful."

William walked out and knew Bakemen was threatening him with Sandra's father. Bakemen picked up the phone.

"This is Bakemen, you keep your eyes and ears open, there might be something special for you if you bring me some good news."

"Yes sir."

"Anything almost out of the ordinary you give me a call."

"Yes sir."

Bakemen hung up, he was sure he had Bradshaw under control now so there were just a couple of calls he need to make, Junior Carposi had set in motion a deal to get rid of Benito Arroyo. Bakemen thought it was over for the Latino motherfuckers when he left Ernesto floating but out of nowhere come his little spick brother but soon he'd be floating also.

Junior was having a hard time the other families didn't respect him like they respected his father. So Junior was pressed to use force when it was collection time. Vincent 'Moon' Moliana had a Meat Market uptown in the Bronx. Vinny also took illegal sports bets for Jimmy 'the Snake' raking in over 250 gees a week but since Junior had taken over Vinny claimed only 20 to 25 gees a week. Of course Junior knew Vinny was shitting him so it was time to take action. The Meat Market was on Gun Hill road two blocks from Evander High School. It was during school hours. Vinny Moon was the last of a dying breed Italians controlling the Bronx. The fucking Jamaicans had taken over shit they sold their weed right in front of his Meat Market and it was as if the Irish Police was just sitting around with donuts stuck up their asses. The bell rang as the door opened. Vinny Moon looked up from cutting his bacon; he couldn't help but suck his teeth seeing the cunt Junior Carposi.

"Junior give me a minute", he said but mumbled,

"You, fuckin prick."

"What was that", Junior asked looking at his man Tony Cheeks.

"I'll be right there."

Business hadn't been good in years' meat wise but the tickets were booming, Vinny Moon was trying to give that to Junior Maybe Jimmy 'the Snake' but not Junior

"Hey Junior let's go in the back and talk", Vinny waved for Junior to follow.

"Cheeks lock the fuckin door", Junior said following Vinny into the back.

"So Junior did you catch that Boston Game?"

"Yeah I had the Knicks by 6."

"The spread was Boston by 10 so I guess you made a killin",

Vinny said with a nervous smile as he pulled out a metal cash box.

"Cut the fuckin bullshit Vinny what the fuck do you have for me this week?"

Vinny opened the metal box and began pulling out stacks of one hundred dollar bills 30 stacks. "Well Junior business hasn't been too good lately you know my people have been scared to come around here."

"Oh yeah Vinny and why is that Vinny", Junior asked beginning to light his cigar.

Vinny looked around nervously,

"th…th…the Jamaicans they sit right in front harassing everyone with their weed."

Junior put his hand in the air stopping Vinny mid-sentence.

"So this is stopping me from collecting my money?" Vinny nodded.

"The Jamaican in front of the store?" Once again Vinny nodded.

"Come here", Junior said to Vinny,

Vinny leaned forward.

"Closer, closer…clooossser." Junior grabbed Vinny by his bloody apron.

"Where the fuck is my money", he said threatening an eye with the cigar.

"This is all I have Junior it's all I got."

"You know what I'm sick of this shit Ralph turn on the meat grinder."

"Oh God Junior no it's all I got please",

Vinny plead as Junior and Cheeks dragged him over to the

meat grinder which whined as Ralph 'the Mouth' hit the power switch.

"Get em",

Junior said to Mouth as he took off his windbreaker jacket and tied the apron around his waist.

"I guess I gotta show you that the Jamaicans are not the ones you should be afraid of give me his hand."

Vinny tried hard to wrestle with Cheek and Ralph but they easily overpowered him. Tears and snot both ran down Vinny Moon's face.

"How bout I feed my dogs Vinny burgers tonight?"

Vinny began to scream as his hand got closer and closer to the blades.

"Now where the fuck is my money?"

"That's all I have Junior I swear."

"Where the fuck is my money?"

"Oh God, Junior oh God okay",

Vinny screamed as his pointer finger touched the blades he finally gave in panting and gasping for air.

"Okay…. Junior, okay." He yelled

"See and you swore, now get my fucking money."

With the tip of his index finger leaking he slid his desk forward pulling up the floor. Junior smiled as he saw the safe. Vinny turned the dial and the safe door popped open.

"Look here", Cheeks said as they looked at over two million dollars.

"500 gees and we're even till next week."

"Your father was a man of respect and honor, you're not even worthy of the name."

"You know what comes with respect Vinny."

(Bang)

"A fuckin bullet, so honestly ask yourself do you want respect? because the next one doesn't have to miss."

Junior and his two henchmen walked out they were about to get into the Cadillac.

"Hold on",

Junior said as he noticed the Jamaicans sitting on the steps next to the Meat Market, Junior approached them,

"A boy way a wan sum weed."

"Nah, nah, do any of you know who I am?"

One of the men sucked his teeth.

"Oh yeah I'm Junior fuckin Carposi and if I hear about anyone of you nappy headed motherfuckers selling weed in front of my place again there's gonna be a fuckin problem".

One of the Rasta's stood up.

"Hush uno pussy hole."

"What did you call me a pussy?"

Junior pulled out his gun, guns came from every direction the same Rasta laugh.

"Pussy hole white boy, go way fi uno dead."

Junior Wasn't stupid he realized he had no wins at the time but he'd be back.

S.T., Adrian and Danger were in the studio, while Adrian was on the phone arguing with Alexis which was all they seemed to do.

"I don't want to hear this shit Lexus there's too much shit goin on to be arguing with you over who I'm fuckin."

"You shouldn't even be dealing with the streets you should be in a multimillion dollar contract with your dumbass."

"When did you start talkin to me like this?"

"When I realized you were so fucking stupid, I gave up everything for you Adrian and you throw everything away, all our dreams you threw it all away for a whore and now she's about to have your baby."

"Is that what this is all about, the baby?"

"Adrian where is she now?"

Adrian didn't want to answer because she was running the streets, which was what she'd been doing the entire pregnancy.

"You can't answer huh, I know you can't she not mother material but fuck her and you I feel sorry for that baby."

While they argued S.T. recorded 'Knock knock who is it them boys that'll get ya.' The engineer Rayzor and Danger just rocked to the music. It was hitting hard but the recording was interrupted by the beeping of S.T.'s pager in the sound booth.

"Dammit Shawn how many times have I told you about taking that thing in the booth now we got to start all over man, fuck."

"Relax Rayzor I'll get it right first shot just let me take care of this really quick."

S.T. put down the headphones and went to the phone. Whoever it was had paged him three more times with 9-11's following the number.

"Hello."

"Yeah somebody paged S.T.?"

"Yeah nigga it's me."

"Now's not a good time."

"Shit I'm in the hospital about to have my baby."

"Come on don't act like you don't know, NOW'S NOT a good time."

"Fuck you", she hung up.

S.T. got back in the sound booth.

"Is your pager off", Rayzor asked.

"Yeah."

"You got everything you need?"

"Yes Rayzor."

"So you're ready."

"Knock knock who is..." S.T. began recording.

Adrian phone rang.

"Yeah."

"Adrian", it was Jessica on the line crying.

"What's wrong mommie?"

"I'm about to have the baby where are you."

"Alexis I call you back", he quickly hung up without a

response.

"What hospital are you at?"

"I'm at Harlem hospital, get over here stupid."

"Okay I'm on my way."

S.T. couldn't hear what was going on outside the booth but he saw Rayzor and Danger hugging Adrian so he knew what was up so he just continued rapping ignoring Adrian. As Adrian walked out the studio he waved to the Feds they in return blew the horn it was going to be like this for a while and they all knew it. Jessica gave birth to an 8 pound 5-ounce little girl Jahnia Walker.

It took almost three hours to finally get Sandra to put on the black dress.

"Oh my God it's a funeral",

Sandra said as apologetic as she could she felt like shit for giving William such a hard time. "Who is it", she now asked.

"Come were late."

They walked up to the service, William was amazed by how many people showed up he was realizing more every day that his sister was more than just a crack head. Nowadays he wasn't sure if she was a crack head at all.

"Oh God William who are these people",

she said now seeming a little nervous seeing the thugs. Now Danger approached, he and William hugged.

"Is this the Misses?"

"Yes", William said.

"Sandra Daniel, Daniel Sandra", he introduced them.

"Nice to meet you", Danger said extending his hand. She accepted,

"Same here."

"Well let me get over her S.T,'s twisted."

William nodded as Danger walked back to comfort his boy.

"Twisted......, what does that mean William, and who are these people?"

After the service William drove to a diner. It was time for William to tell her everything. And that's just what he did he told everything from Phillip paying his tuition selling drugs to put him through school. How he was now incarcerated doing 25 to life he told about Monica how she had basically raised him while his parents worked two and three shift. He told who S.T. was then Danger and Adrian.

"Oh my God so these are the people you've been running

around with all times of night William." He nodded.

"Please tell me you're not involved with selling drugs."

"No, No, hell no…. Sandra you know me better than that."

"William I don't know anything about you, we've been together for seven years, and now I found out you have a brother and sister, so if you're not selling drugs how did you get mixed up with these guys?"

Now he had to tell about Bakemen's corruption, how he was the one of the biggest drug suppliers in New York, how he believed Bakemen was responsible for Commissioner Donahue's as well as Monica's death. How Bakemen continuously threatened his career but now he was too deep in to walk away. It was Bakemen having women call the house at night.

"Oh my God it's all my fault William I pushed you and pushed you to go work for this man, I'm so sorry."

All William could do was shake his head; it was so much deeper than that.

"It wasn't you Sandra he gave me no choice he threatened you and your parents."

"My parents." "

What's worse is Jefferson plays golf with him every weekend."

"You have to tell my dad."

"No Sandra."

"William are you crazy? my family is in danger"

"Look we have to continue like everyday life, as soon as Bakemen see's anything out of the ordinary he might react."

"So what are you going to do?"

"Danger, excuse me Daniel and I are working on that now don't worry."

It was easy to say don't worry but neither Danger nor William had any idea what they would should or could do, William just knew Bakemen had to pay for everything.

Word quickly spread about the incident between Junior Carposi and Vinny 'Moon' Moliana. With the mob weakening the other families felt they needed to stand together to fight against the Spanish, Irish, Russians and Jamaicans. The Rizzoto family and the Corleone's were pissed. Moon was a made man and if he would have died Junior was as good as dead. The families sat around the table to discuss how Junior would be dealt with. Vinny Moon sat there with his hand bandage.

"Don this fuck Junior Carposi is outta control",

Tommy Carpone said to Don Rizzoto.

"You guys gotta understand I've been paying him every week for a year he has no respect", Vinny Moon added.

"What are you paying him for",

Don Rizzoto asked in his raspy almost a whisper voice.

"Protection but honestly, the only protection I need is from him", Vinny Moon said as woeful as he could.

IN DANGER'S EYES

"Don't worry about Junior Carposi. I'll handle him", Don Rizzoto said in his loudest whisper. "What I want to know is what's going on with Stagalini and the fuckin Irish pig Bakemen." Everyone was quiet; Don slammed his hand on the table.

No one can tell me anything about Stagalini", his word fading before his sentence finished. "Bakemen is."

"Fuck Bakemen find Stagalini I…want his fucking tongue on this table… Damone get fuckin Carposi here before the sun goes down",

Don Rizzoto took a deep breath before continuing.

"Bakemen's days are numbered…the Feds are on him…just like us. I want everybody on the up and up", he paused to sip his beverage.

"They're about to hit and…I want my boy clean."

In New York Don Rizzoto was the head of all families and in 1992 what he said went there were no if ands or buts about it. He said he wanted everyone on the up and up and that's how it would be. No dope deals no shake downs no nothing, all businesses would continue. The garbage trucks, the off track betting, the gentlemen clubs and well as the bookies but under no circumstances would anyone be involved in murder, extortion, drug dealing or assault. Damone was Don Rizzoto's oldest son and heir to the family name; he wasn't foolish like Junior he understood that the way to control shit was to have the others respect to make enemies on the families was sealing your own fate. Don Rizzoto biggest problem was Stagalini as Jimmy 'the Snakes', Underboss. Stagalini had a little too much information which was detrimental to all the families if he were to testify so Don Rizzoto wanted him permanently hushed, first things first.

It was little after 5:30 pm when Carposi, Ralph 'the Mouth' and Tony Cheeks walked into Don Rizzoto Office.

"Don Rizzoto", Junior said with a respect he lacked for everyone else.

"Sit the fuck down", Rizzoto said in a low whisper which was meant to be a scream but seemed to be a little more frightening.

"Was I talkin to you two fucks",

Don Rizzoto said in the direction of Mouth and Cheeks who both jumped up. Junior just sat there like a child knowing he was about to be grounded, Rizzoto took a deep breath to strength his low voice.

"Who the fuck...do you think", a breath, "You, fuckin idiot", a breath.

"Boss", Carposi tried to say something,

"Shut the fuck", a breath, "up when I want...you to say something...I'll tell you...what the fuck to say."

Junior just sat there with his head down.

"I love your father, I pray he'll be home soon but you little...fuck",

Rizzoto took a sip from his glass.

"You will not...ruin what your dad...built...You will not collect a...fuckin red cent in this country...without talking to...me first am I understood?"

Junior nodded his head, the non-verbal agreement pissed Don Rizzoto off he jumped up.

"Do you understand", his voice barely rising but spit flying across the table into Junior's face.

"Yes" Junior said wiping the saliva off his face.

"Please dad calm down let me talk to Junior, Jimmy come on", Damone said leading Junior out of the office.

They walked out to the veranda Mouth and cheeks right behind them.

"Jimmy you have to excuse my dad he's under a lot of stress if you would have made the meeting earlier you'd know what's going on." Junior sucked his teeth.

"Your dads yelling like I'm the enemy when we got these spicks and niggers moving into our neighborhoods everyday taking food out of our kids mouths, what the fuck did I do that was so horrible?"

"Vincent Moliana."

"Vinny Moon."

"Yeah Jimmy he's a made man and you put his hand in a meat grinder",

Damone said with a smile, Junior respected Damone not just because they were close to the same age Damone was 25 while Junior was 20 but Damone also showed him respect he called him Jimmy. Damone was one of the only men in the families to show him that respect.

"Come on Damone Vinny Moon's a fuckin prick."

"I agree", Damone said,

"But nevertheless he's a made man."

"Well when my dad put me in charge he made me a boss."

"Jimmy that's a whole nother argument which I can't disagree with but you gotta respect the don's rules which reminds me, that prick Stags is still hiding out, we don't know what he told the Feds but they're on us heavy so nothing."

"What do you mean?"

"You know just what I mean Jimmy no dope no nothing we can't afford indictments so stay under the radar." Junior nodded his agreement.

Junior and his two men walked to their car, Damone opened the door and stepped outside.

"Jimmy." Junior stopped in his tracks turned to face the man who would one day be king.

"Yeah."

"No nothing", Damone said once again.

"I got it."

Cheeks opened the car door and Junior climbed in the back seat.

"What should we do Boss",

Ralph asked as they headed off the Don's property. Junior bit his lip trying to control his anger as they drove through the estate gates he exploded punching the back of the seat.

"Mother fuckin bitch faggot motherfucker, cunt prick bastard."

"You alright Boss", Cheeks asked.

"Yeah, yeah."

"What are we gonna do", Cheeks asked.

"Business as usual."

"But the Don", Ralph started.

"Fuck Rizzoto he's a fuckin dead man you hear me he's a fuckin dead man."

"But I thought you and Damone were close?"

"I ain't talkin about Damone."

"The Don", Ralph asked. Junior nodded.

"But if you kill Rizzoto"

"Exactly", was all Junior said his mind was made up by killing Rizzoto he could make his move to be Boss.

Jahnia was a month old and Adrian was mister mom as Jessica somehow found her way into every party stitches in her ass still fresh. Danger and S.T. sat in the V.I.P. section sipping Moet. "Damn where the fuck is A", S.T. asked.

"I don't know but here comes drunk ass Jessica", Danger answered.

Neither of them knew why they were at the Manhattan party, Budda Bless was performing by now Budda should have known Danger had nothing to do with him being shot.

"Hey Niggas can I get a drink", Jessica said stumbling into the V.I.P. section.

"Looks like you had enough to drink", Danger said.

"Yeah you need to be home with your baby", S.T. added.

"Shit my baby home with her daddy and I'm too young and beautiful to be sitting at home acting like a happy housewife you know, shit nigga I need to get my party on", she said sitting down on S.T. lap pulling a Britney Spears flashing Danger her bare vagina.

"Maybe you shouldn't have had a baby if you weren't ready to be a mother."

"Nigga listen I'm living, shit Alexis could be his Susie home maker, fuck that either ya'll poppin bottles or not."

Danger was disgusted this was the nasty bitch Adrian left Alexis to have a child with.

"Well you could get to steppin cause ain't nobody poppin nothing with you."

"Fuck ya'll where the real niggas at shit S.T. you gonna want some of this ass soon."

She got up and walked away. That was the first time Danger noticed D-Most and Budda Bless sitting across the room. Jessica went over to them and sat down. Budda just sat there screw facing Danger. Danger was tempted to walk over but with Jessica over there that moment wasn't a good time.

It was after 3 am when Budda took the stage.

"Yeah is Brooklyn in the house", the crowd went crazy.

"Is the Bronx in this Bitch?" Again the crowd went crazy.

"Yeah, Yeah, there's some lovely ladies, out here tonight, yeah I might find my wife in here. Manhattan definitely got it goin on, I also see a lot of bitch ass niggas, ya'll may know a few months ago I got shot up the kid is good",

The beat began to play low in the background.

"Haters can't stop the boy but I got one thing to say Booyaka Booyaka Booyaka on yo bitch ass."

It was Budda's latest single which was tearing the club up. In the past both Budda and S.T. had mentioned names in their songs as of late they had stopped especially after the shooting. There were just subliminal messages in the lyrics. In the particular song Budda asked are you from BK or Harlem damn son why you dick ridin as he finished he started another joint for the girls

"Ya boy's wife is a Hoe". Jessica loved it.

The party was over everyone crowded around outside.

Danger and S.T. sat on the hood of his Benz surrounded by women.

"You ready", Danger asked S.T.

"Nah man you see all this pussy man chill."

"That's your problem, you always stuck on pussy don't you know there's this thing called Aids nigga?"

"Man Danger that shits for dope fiends and faggots."

Just then shots rang out people scattered jumping in cars hitting the deck and just running this way and that way. S.T. and Danger dove into the Benz desperately trying to see who it was shooting and to their surprise it was Budda Bless standing atop his Land Cruiser shooting in the air.

It was that night Budda Bless hooked up with his team the Renegades with this group Budda Bless would literally push his career to the maximum. Bad boy media coverage being blamed for shit he had nothing to do with taking charges for his boys. One of his boys shot an off duty cop. Two weeks later Budda was caught with the pistol he would take the case to trial due to the witness statement Budda won trial after that he was unstoppable movie deals and everything. If the entertainment business negative publicity seemed to be the best Budda would go on to be one of the highest ever grossing artist in hip-hop.

Almost three months had passed the team began to get restless. No one was hustling, everyone was eating off of S.T.'s show and they were literally burning him out three and four shows a week and he was only getting 2 gees a show. Meanwhile Budda Bless was starring in his first Move Ice Water he had two albums out and three videos on the top ten. It seemed as if getting shot was the best thing to ever happen to him. Sources said he had over million in Jewelry he literally had rap in the chokehold. And no one could tell him anything.

S.T. hated Budda's success he truly believed Budda was living his life, and he thought of every angle to try and get back on track with Budda including getting shot.

"Nigga are you crazy", Adrian yelled as S.T. told his plan.

"It worked for Budda look at what he's doin movies and shit."

"Don't worry something big is about to happen we really about to make moves just hold ya head and be easy stop talkin crazy, you told Danger that shit?"

"Nah."

"and you better not S sometimes I wonder if you smoking the shit we supposed to be selling",

both men laughed as S. T's pager beeped he looked at the number.

"I need a pay phone." S.T. said,

"Here."

Adrian passed him his new cellular phone which was the

size of a brick.

"Nah", S.T. answered nervously,

"I need a payphone."

Adrian pulled over as S.T. got out to use the pay phone. Adrian decided to call Jessica her line didn't pick up. Adrian knew she was mad that she had to stay home with the baby so he figured that's why she didn't answer so he dialed Alexis, no matter what she was always there for him. "What you doin", he asked.

"I was thinkin about Jahnia and you."

She truly loved Adrian and he truly loved her. She just prayed that he would wake up before it was too late.

Earlier That Night

The black sedan sat parked across the street from Palosi one of the best Italian Restaurant in New York City. The three men patiently waited they had been sitting there for almost an hour and 45 minutes as the fat sloppy Italian sat inside with his two bodyguards and a business associate Malcome Geradi an accountant from Jersey. They discussed the sanitation business over linguini and fettuccine and it was becoming very prosperous. Don Rizzoto was about to become part owner of the biggest trucking company in Berger County New Jersey and all it would cost the Boss was 37 gees which was peanuts. So they shook hands and sipped some wine to celebrate it wasn't everyday a man brought into a million dollar a year business for less than 1 percent.

The accountant was the first to walk out.

"Finally",

The man in the back seat said as they began to load their weapons. From where they were parked they could see the entire corridor.

"Put on the hats", he now said from the back seat.

"Boss these are the ugliest hats I've ever seen"

"Shut the fuck up and put on the hat"

They all put on the round mink hats.

"There he is", the driver said,

The weapons were locked and loaded, they jumped out and slowly walked across the street. In all black hats and black fur trench coats. They stood in front of the building next to Palosi's; the man from the back seat lit a cigarette. Don Rizzoto's driver pulled up but he was no threat at all, he was just a driver.

First the biggest bodyguard walked out, looking up and down the street nodding in the direction of the men out enjoying their cigarettes. Next the second bodyguard followed by Rizzoto. The door was opened. The man from the back seat tossed his cigarette and grabbed two browning nine millimeters off his waist, the other two followed his, lead Don Rizzoto was almost in the car, he spotted the hit men before his bodyguards. Taking a deep breath, he whizzed,

"The Russians."

(Rat tat tat tat) (bang bang bang) (Rat tat tat tat) (Bang Bang)

All the men emptied their clips killing Don Rizzoto his body guards and his driver.

The next morning Brooklyn police were called to an apartment building in Howard Beach. While cleaning the corridors the superintendent noticed the door open. He knew the tenants to be very secretive so he found this strange, he first opened the door calling out,

"Hello it's the super",

He called out still knocking very hard, still no answer, he walked in to investigate the premises, it was his job. It was daytime and the apartment was so dark the super couldn't see his hand in front of his face. The occupants had painted the windows black, and the entire apartment had been sound proof as if a music studio, but The floor. He slipped and grabbed on to the wall, it was wet and, and slippery. There was an odor of something burning in the air, not like a fire burning but more like a fire crackers had been set off. The Super walked into the kitchen, he fondled the walls trying to find something to hold on to keep his balance the marble floor was like ice.

"Whoa",

He screamed as he went down hard he moaned in pain from that fall he crawled to the window it was too slippery to try to get up whatever was on the floor was all over him now he tugged at the thick foam padding at the window after a struggle it finally came down. The man screamed as he realized the liquid on the floor was blood, he jumped to his feet slipping and sliding as if he had ice skates on through a seen he only describes as a slaughterhouse. Screaming he ran out of the apartment,

"Call the police call the police, please someone call Police."

Banging on every door getting everyone out the building.

The police arrived onto the scene to find what they believed to be five men. Body parts where scattered all over the apartment, it would take year maybe decades to find a fingerprint. It took officers almost 3 days to collect body parts in the puzzle. They also recovered guns three black trench coat and 2 mink hats.

When Damone Rizzoto called the meeting of the bosses he never intended on Junior being there.

Junior Carposi walked in with an entirely new arrogance as he walked in and sat in Don Rizzoto's seat then put his feet on the desk. The other bosses were appalled.

"What the fuck is this, the most powerful men in the Tri-State area. and you guys don't invite me",

Junior said smiling as he bit into an apple he took from the centerpiece.

"Jimmy don't come in here disrespecting my father. You came in here like",

In the middle of Damone's sentence Junior pulled out a bloodied hat and threw it on the table in the direction of Vinny 'Moon' Moliana, getting speckles of blood on his suit. The men at the table jumped back.

"Damone I love you like a brother, we've grown up together, I have the utmost love and respect for you, and your family......but today your father is dead, and so are the men that killed him."

"What", Damone Rizzoto said standing.

"Everyone at this table is a made man except you", Damone started.

"My Fuckin Parents are full blood Sicilian. If you

motherfuckers aren't gonna make me, I'll make myself, any of you men test me and ya dead.... you hear me dead! Every fuckin one of you. There's a new Don in fuckin town and either it's my way or goodbye. So I think you guys should decide right here and now, because I'm ready for war."

Everyone could tell Junior Carposi was serious but no one was ready to test his words. It would be the first time in the history of the Mafia that an unmade man took control. One by one they walked over bowed their heads and kissed the ring that once belonged to his father. Junior had done what his father had been afraid to do, he murdered Don Rizzoto, framed and murdered their biggest competition, Chevchenko and the Russian mob boss. Then used intimidation to take control of New York.

The Bullet Proof Don, Don Carposi it was definitely a start of the ending for the New York and New Jersey Mafia. Right away phone calls were made to alert every one of the news 21-year-old Don Carposi was now in control. Men instantly packed their belongings, no one wanted to be under the asshole but some had no choice either leave or stay and obey. Jimmy 'the Snake' was pissed and Junior wouldn't accept any of his calls, he couldn't believe the blatant disrespect Junior had showed to everyone he was ready to put a hit out on his own son.

Another man totally pissed with the move was Stags. Stagalini knew New York was finished. He definitely had to get out of the state now. He knew with Junior Carposi was in charge he was a dead man. Every henchman in the tri-state would be looking for him now. His heart pounded as the phone rang

"Come on pick up, pick up."

"Good Morning William Bradshaw Attorney General's office."

"Yes hello is Bradshaw in?"

"Yes whose calling?"

"Look Miss I just need Bradshaw."

"I'm sorry sir but I cannot bother him unless I know whose calling."

"Tell him Reggie Stags." Lisa Morning quickly punched the call through,

"Mr. Bradshaw you have a Reggie Stags on the line."

"Fuck, send it through."

"Bradshaw."

"Stagalini are you out of your fucking mind calling this office?"

"Look you gotta do something Bradshaw, the waters getting deep, and I'm not about to sit here and drown."

"What are you talking about?"

"You know Don Rizzoto was gunned down."

"Yeah by the Russians."

"Hmmm, guess again." There was a short pause.

"No", Bradshaw finally said.

"Yes."

"Are you telling me Junior did the hit?"

"Yes so now you know, I have to get the fuck outta here."

"Do you know the White Plains area",

Bradshaw gave Stagalini the address to a little café in White Plains New York he quickly cleared his desk unaware of what he was going to do but he knew something had to be done.

"Bakemen."

"Yes who's this?"

"Lisa."

"Good Morning Mrs. Mornings what do you have?"

"Reginald Stagalini just called William",

Lisa explained everything she had overheard.

"Lisa you're the greatest, there'll be something a little extra in your bosses' mailbox for you", Bakemen quickly hung up and called Detective Lipsett.

"Sonny its Bakemen."

"Yeah Boss."

"I hate when you do that."

"Sorry boss", Lipsett said being sarcastic.

"Listen Sonny WB might be on the move I want him erased but it must look accidental." "Gotcha."

"Sonny."

"Yes boss."

"It has to look like an accident."

"Got it boss."

As Detective Lipsett and his partner Beckett headed to the State building Bakemen called Junior Carposi to let him know that Stags had resurfaced. Junior also sent two men to follow Bradshaw.

Bradshaw was smarter than the men following him, maybe it was because he also had street knowledge. One thing he knew for sure was it was more than the Feds following him but maybe that would be the reason he'd be safe with the Feds on his ass. They wouldn't allow him to get hurt, even he had to laugh, they had been watching Donahue and his entire family had been murdered, and of course they had to be watching Don Rizzoto maybe he wasn't safe.

"Shit",

Bradshaw said out loud, he was gonna need help on this one. He pulled over to a pay phone he knew his cellular phone was being tapped. He was already nervous and pissed that Stagalini had called his office, no telling how many people had heard his conversation.

"Daniel I need your help."

"Where are you?"

"125th."

"137th and Lenox there's an ice cream parlor meet me there."

Bradshaw hung up the pay phone looking around nervously, he tried to spot his followers but everyone looked suspicious. So Bradshaw nonchalantly got into his car and drove up to 137th. Danger was standing outside. Bradshaw got out and Danger shook his hand cameras went off.

"What's wrong", Danger asked.

"I got a call from Stagalini, Junior Carposi's the Don now."

"Get the fuck outta here."

"Yeah so everyone, including your team…. are in deep shit."

"So what do you want to do?"

Finally, Bradshaw had an idea he explained it to Danger who stood there nodding, he liked the plan.

"Let's go",

Danger said knowing they were being watched the first stop was Adrian and Jessica's house. Without hesitation Adrian was ready he and Danger jumped in one car as Bradshaw went his way. Detective Lipsett gave a call to Junior he needed a car at the address. Twenty minutes later a car was there to watch the house. Bradshaw was headed across to Westchester he watched his rearview intensively he was hoping they were following him, actually he needed them to be following him.

Meanwhile Adrian and Danger fully loaded went to pick up the package.

"Danger since when did we begin fucking with the other side", Adrian asked.

Danger couldn't help but to laugh.

"You know A, Williams is one of us and somehow if I could start over I'd probably have gone your route or his."

That was the first time Adrian actually thought about what he had given up. His dreams, Alexis dreams and now he was in the middle of a war against the mob and the police. How the fuck could three brothers from the hood take on politicians, crooked cops and the mafia? Damn he should be in Miami right now. Tarry Town New York.

"I don't think anyone followed us",

Danger said as he pulled into the driveway of the address Bradshaw gave him. They walked up to the door together with Adrian knocking at the door. Seconds later a voice asked,

"Who is it?" Danger replied,

"Bradshaw sent us", the door opened. Danger stood face to face with Stags who shook his head, "Oh God Bradshaw sent the street thugs protect me."

"Hey, you can save yourself for all I care", Adrian answered.

Stags laughed moving aside.

"Come in", Stags said.

"I gotta grab a few things.

Bradshaw pulled up he just sat there for a moment not knowing what he was going to say. Although he saw no one, he knew he had been followed and he began to second guess his choice to come here. He didn't know if he was putting himself or the people close to him in danger. He thought about Sandra and when he first met her, he thought about school and his first case he ever won. Now here he was in the midst of a federal investigation. The Mafia was waiting for the right moment to attack him and for the first time in 15 years it was the streets of Harlem that had his back thinking about Adrian and Danger brought tears to his eyes because they made him think of Monica and how he ignored his family. Afraid of his high class associates realizing he, wasn't anything but a poor negro from the ghetto that made it.

He put on his Cartier framed sunglasses and looked around. The sunglasses were also to hide the swollen red eyes from his crying. He approached the door still hesitant on what he was going to do so he faked ringing the doorbell then turned to watch the street. A few cars passed the Crestwood Manor one of the nicer neighborhoods in Westchester. Nothing too suspicious. William took a deep breath.

"Fuck it", he said to himself as he finally rang the bell.

The little toy poodle began to alert the residents that someone was at the door. William patiently waited with his back to the door watching the street. The door opened and

William turned around.

"William what are you doing way out here and where is Sandra?"

"Sandra's probably at her spinning class, I need to speak to Jefferson he wouldn't be here would he?"

"Come in he's in his study, would you like some tea?"

"No thank you I just need to see Jefferson and I'll be leaving." Ellen walked off towards the kitchen.

William headed in the direction of Jefferson's study, he could hear him on the phone.

"Si hombre es Benito."

It shocked William to hear Jefferson speaking Spanish. William knocked.

"Hold on, who is it."

"It's William."

"Oh Christ Benito I'll give you a call back it's my son in-law, yes I know I know 7 pm Tuesday alright I'll talk to you later, come in."

William entered the study.

"Bradshaw."

"Jefferson."

"Well how can I help you Bradshaw?",

Jefferson asked gesturing for William to have a seat, William sat down as if releasing tons of stress.

"I'm in a bit of a jam Jefferson and I don't know what to do." Jefferson pulled out a box of cigars.

He extended the smokes to Bradshaw, seeing the box and even the brand made him think about Bakemen's office, maybe Bakemen had given them to Jefferson. William took a cigar lit it and began to explain what was going on, everything never blinking never looking away. Jefferson held on to every word it even helped ease a little of William's stress as Jefferson nodded as if he understood. Every threat, every deal, every contract, even the threats to Jefferson himself.

"This Bakemen sounds like a dangerous man Bradshaw, why didn't you tell me about your sister?"

"I was ashamed of that side of my family. I'm sure you can understand."

"Listen Bradshaw don't worry I have friends in the Feds you can be sure that Sandra and I are safe you just make sure your safe. You do what you have to do, I call my friends to make sure you're not in any trouble, what you can do is tell me where your taking Stagalini maybe the Feds will be able to protect him."

William didn't know where Adrian and Danger would take Stags so he told Jefferson he would get back to him.

"Do you have a weapon", Jefferson asked.

"Yes."

"Is it legal?"

"No I got it from Adrian."

"We'll give it to me what's wrong with you; you're a professional man you can't get caught like some boy in the hood."

Jefferson was right he gave the nine millimeter to Jefferson.

"You have a reputation to uphold I will take care of these problems you just don't do anything foolish."

William walked out he wondered if he had told Jefferson too much, maybe not because Jefferson had political friends that would be able to help him. Smoking the cigar awaked an urge in William that he hadn't had in years. He opened up the glove compartment and pulled out an unopened pack of cigarettes he lit one to help calm his nerves.

When Bakemen took the call from Carlos he knew it couldn't be anything good.

"Carlos how are you?"

"Answer one question for me."

"Yes."

"Are you in control of your affairs?"

"Yes."

"So why am I sitting here listening to this cunts sob stories, if you cannot handle things I will put someone in your position that can."

"I will handle it", Bakemen said in a frustrated tone.

"Am I upsetting you", Carlos asked.

"No", Bakemen answered.

"Are you sure because if I am I would want you to tell me because if my name comes up none of you assholes will have to worry about jail do you understand me",

there was silence on the other line.

"Do you understand me Bakemen?"

"Yes", Bakemen finally answered.

"Don't worry about our friend I've sent my people to handle him."

"So handle."

(Click)

Carlos had hung up. Bakemen sat there with the phone in

his hand he dialed Ralph 'the Mouth'. "Where are you", Bakemen asked.

"Still sitting at the apartment in Harlem."

"Why", Bakemen screamed into the receiver.

The Mouth got quiet he didn't know what to say.

"I asked you a fucking question."

"Well Junior told me to watch this apartment in case they brought Stagalini back here."

"So who's following Bradshaw?"

"Junior and Cheeks", Bakemen hung up and quickly called Junior's car phone.

Junior answered himself. A few months ago Bakemen would have yelled and screamed all types of obscenities at Junior but now he was the Don which merited the utmost respect.

"Junior what happened to Bradshaw?"

"We followed him to a mansion in Crestwood turns out it was his father in-laws place."

"I could have told you that! Just leave him, Carlos has sent his own men."

"What Harper I want this Moolie bastard."

"Listen Junior grow up this is business not your personal

revenge escapade, now pull off of him, Bradshaw's not picking up Stagalini."

"How do you know that", Junior asked.

Bakemen could only roll his eyes at the stupidity of Junior this was the man in charge of the New York Mafia it was definitely doomed.

"Is he headed back to New York City?"

"Yes."

"Well we know Stags is not in the city he's somewhere in Westchester and while you have Mouth watching the running backs house it's the running back that getting Stags so pull off of Bradshaw and get me the fucking running back", Bakemen hung up.

Junior was still upset he wanted Bradshaw bad but at that particular moment what Carlos said went but not for long. Carlos didn't know it but even his days were numbered sooner or later. Junior knew he would meet the man and when he did, it would be time for him to take a dirt nap. Junior dial the number two rings he picked up.

"Boss what's up?"

"Get the girl", was all Junior said.

Looking in the rearview mirror was the only way William could drive. Nowadays he barely watched the road ahead of him he watched everything around him. He saw a Bronco coming up fast but he really paid it no mind until it was too late. It rammed the back of his Lincoln several times. He swerved fighting to catch control of the car as over and over the Bronco smashed into him.

"What the fuck?",

William screamed as the driver of the Bronco pushed him into the guardrail. William stepped on the gas pedal pulling away from the Bronco. It pulled back up quick and William tried to swerve to avoid the hit.

Still the Bronco grazed the back fender sending the Lincoln into a fishtail. The Lincoln swayed from one side of the parkway to the other finally spinning out of control. The car careened into a ditch flipping three or four times. The Bronco stopped. The driver saw no movement so he pulled off while cars slowly passed. People were looking but no one stopping to help. William struggled with his seatbelt as he coughed and gasped for air. He finally got the seatbelt off. The car was flipped upside down so when he snapped free he fell, pulling himself out of the wrecked car and grabbing the pack of cigarettes he, sat on the side of the road holding his bleeding head. He laughed as he thought about being followed by the Feds.

"Well where the fuck are you now", he asked out loud to no one.

Just then a gray Crown Victoria pulled over. Two Agents got out.

"William Bradshaw", William nodded.

"Are you alright?"

"Yeah I guess, took a bump on my head."

"Well we need you to come with us."

"For what?"

"You're in danger."

"You think so", William said sarcastically looking back at his Lincoln.

"We have no time to joke please get in."

Bradshaw got into the car. He knew right away he would say nothing. As they arrived at One Federal Plaza William turned off both his pager and his phone. They sat him in a room no cuffs or anything; he wasn't under arrest or anything. They just had a few questions to ask him. William lit another cigarette just then the door opened and two different Agents walked in one carrying a folder.

"Mr. Bradshaw I'm Agent Spence and this is my partner Agent Fredrick", said the one carrying the folder, as he tossed the beige folder on the desk in front of him.

"I just have a few questions for you Bradshaw."

"I don't know anything", William replied to Spence

"Now just a second how do you know if I don't ask you", Spence said calmly.

This was strange to William he had never been on this side before.

"First things first Bradshaw someone wants you dead do you have any idea who?"

William took a long pull on his cigarette then stubbed it out in the ashtray.

"You guys have been following me for weeks, I figured you'd know." Spence's facial expression never changed.

"Do you know who this is",

Spence asked shoving a picture of a young black man in front of William. William looked but didn't recognize the face so he shook his head no.

"Have you ever heard of Decons", Fredrick finally spoke.

"Yes, I've tried to find indictments on them a few years back"

"So you ought to know that man", Spence asked again.

William carefully examined the photo again.

"should I?"

"Yes."

"Who is he?", William asked with a genuine curiosity.

"This is Lance Palmer, does the name ring a bell." William shook his head no.

"He's the number two man in the Decons street gang"
Agent Spence paused for a moment.

"I find it a little funny Mr. Bradshaw that at one point in
your career you were planning on taking down the Decons
but now you tell me you don't know one of its head
members." "Honestly Agent Spence as soon as I became
DA I was told to focus on Jimmy 'the Snake' Carposi."

"I see so you know who this is", Spence threw another
photo in front of William.

"Junior Carposi", William answered.

"And how about these", now Spence threw several pictures
of William with Danger.

"Do you know who this is?",

Now Spence pointed to Danger, William nodded his head.

"Who is he?", Fredrick asks.

"Daniel Warren", William answered.

"And what does he do for a living?", Fredrick now asked.

"He's CEO of I-ACOCA Records." Spence smiled the
statement upset Fredrick.

"So how long has the Attorney General been associated
with drug dealers?", Spence asked.

"I find it funny that it took you what seven years to make
Attorney General you must know some powerful people",

Spence added.

"Daniel 'Danger' Warren is the lead man in the Decons and I'm sitting here with several pictures of the both of you. What the fuck is going on!" Fredrick was now screaming.

"I don't know where you're getting your information Agent."

"Let's cut the bullshit Bradshaw do you sell drugs?"

"No."

"Are you helping I-ACOCA Records launder money?"

"No."

"Is Bakemen corrupt?"

"I don't know."

"Who's Carlos?"

William said nothing.

"So you don't know Carlos", Fredrick asked.

"I know my rights, am I under arrest?"

"No Bradshaw." William stood up.

"Then I can leave?" Spence nodded.

"The only way we can help you, is if you help us."

"Yeah well you've been following me for months."

"Years", Frederick added.

"And", William said pointing to the scar on his head,

"Where were you when I needed you?"

"I promise you we'll be there from now on."

"Yeah that's good to know", William got up and headed for the door.

He was pissed he was involved even deeper than he thought and why wouldn't Daniel tell him about his connection to Decons then again William realized he never asked. Now the feds were asking him about the man who was only known as Carlos. William only knew the name never saw the face or heard a voice. As soon as William got outside he used a pay phone to call Daniel.


You can take a brother out the hood but you can't take the hood out a brother. Out of state out of danger supposed to be laying low with over 100 gees stashed. No reason to be involved in any crime, L.P. went out to Oklahoma and brought a fake ID and was living as Duane Jackson. He got a little job in a bar just to stay out of trouble. He had been out there for two months, but trouble had a way of finding L.P. It was a Thursday night D.J. as his co-workers called him was sweeping and that's when he noticed the red head sitting by herself.

"Hey mommy what's good Red", he said, she smiled.

"Hey", she said bashfully.

"Damn girl is it Red everywhere?"

"Boy you ain't from these parts", she said in her southern drawl.

"Nah baby Brooklyn New York but what's good?"

"What you mean?"

"I want to get to know you."

The 19 year old red head just blushed and smiled intrigued by the New York accent.

"Why you wanna know me?"

"Cause you look good I wanna see your other red hair."

Once again Red just laughed.

"You here by yourself", L.P. asked.

"No."

"Who you with?"

"My boyfriend", she said pointing to the big red faced Hillbilly.

"D.J.", the owner called to him.

"Yeah Boss."

"Please leave the customers alone."

"Boss she wants it", L.P. Laughed as he told his boss

. "She's here with someone just leave her alone she's trouble."

The boss had warned him and L.P. stayed away constantly winking and blowing kisses make her blush and smile a couple of times up until her Hillbilly boyfriend caught her. The bar was closing L.P. was outside sitting on his Benz smoking a joint.

"Hey Buddy", the Hillbilly called as he stood there with one of his big Hillbilly friends.

"You talkin to me?", L.P. asked the 6 foot 4 inch 285 pound redneck.

"Yeah", the Hillbilly said walking towards him.

"Leave him alone baby", Red yelled from the Hillbillies pickup truck.

"No Susie this high class nigger needs to be taught a lesson on respect."

"Whoa, whoa who the fuck you callin nigga?"

"You boy."

(Pow)

The hillbilly hit him, L.P. had never seen stars before he couldn't remember the last time he'd been hit. He tried to regain his composure then (Pow) the Hillbilly hit him again.

"Baby stop", L.P. heard Red scream again.

"Shut up girl, bet you won't"

(Paw)

"flirt with my"

(Paw)

"woman again."

L.P. was on his back, he couldn't believe it he'd survived Bronxville and Bedstuy now here he was put on his back by a fucking farmer.

"Leave alone Jed", the other hillbilly said,

"He's had enough."

"You hear boy watch what you say to men's women."

The Hillbilly walked over ready to help L.P. to his feet. L.P. spit blood in the man's face Jed flipped and began stomping L.P. L.P. slowly reached into his boot and pulled out a 32 revolver Jed hadn't realized it.

"Jed Baby", Red screamed as she saw the gun Jed turned to run

(Bang, Bang).

L.P. hit Jed in his leg dropping him; Red began to scream

as Jed's friend ran back into the bar. As Jed began to beg
for his life a L.P. beaten badly, face bloody and swollen
struggled to his feet.

"Mother…fucker", he said spitting blood on the pavement.

"Please leave him alone", Red screamed.

(Bang) L.P. fired a shot at her but missed, he now stood
over the Hillbilly who tried to beg (Bang, Bang)

his last two shots hit Jed in the face killing him instantly.

A cracked rib, slight concussion and punctured lung…. L.P.
passed out behind the wheel of his car. He woke up 3 days
later bandaged up and handcuffed to a hospital bed. Three
weeks out of New York and Lance Palmer was under arrest
for the murder of Jed Bunker, the attempted murder of
Susan Garth and false impersonation. Two months later he
was sitting in a holding cell being interrogated by Federal
Agent Kramer Spence.

"It was Daniel Warren man I swear he made me kill Kevin
'King James' and he made me shoot the rapper."

"What else can you tell me about Daniel Warren?"

"He's the leader of the Decons oh and he just hooked up
with the crooked lawyer Wilson Brad something."

"William Bradshaw", Spence corrected him.

"Yeah, yeah that's it."

Danger knew Harlem was hot so the safest place for them to hide Stags was uptown at Josephine's. William took the bus to the train then a cab just to make sure he wasn't being followed he arrived at Josephine's a little after 7 pm.

"Damn you look like shit",

Stags told William who began to tell about the car accident which led to him yelling in Danger's face.

"Why didn't you tell me you were the head man of the Decons."

Adrian and Danger both laughed.

"You find this shit funny I'm connected to a street gang"

"Relax", Danger said to William.

"Listen man I was born and raised in Harlem Decon's is out of Brooklyn and you of all people should know that."

William thought about it, he had investigated Decons for a few weeks so he knew that was true he then began to explain his interrogation by the Feds.

Just then Adrian's cell phone rang he answered the star tech,

"Hello."

"Hey Mister Running Back."

"Who the fuck is this?"

"Mister running back you have something I want."

"Oh yeah suck my dick faggot."

"Whoa, whoa such harsh words running back, maybe this will change your mind."

Seconds later.

"Baby help me", the sobbing voice whined.

"Now can we talk business?" the voice asked.

"Who is this? I swear."

"You swear what? This is Junior Carposi and I want that rat bastard Stagalini. Now I'll give you a chance to talk it over with your boys just remember give me what I want and nothing happens to this hot piece of ass", Carposi hung up.

"What's wrong with you?", Danger asked.

"Carposi called me."

"What happen?", William now asked.

"He has Jessica he wants Stagalini."

Everyone was quiet, the pressure was on and something had to be done. Finally, Danger had an idea it was time to get everyone together, for some reason they couldn't't find S.T. They needed a few guns and a little more back up, it was time to test what started as friendships. By himself

Danger drove to the other side of the Bronx it had been over two months. Danger heard on the streets things had changed. Somehow Benny Yayo was working with Junior Carposi, Danger prayed it was just a rumor but 6 times out of 10 if the streets said it, then it was true. It was a little after 11 am when Danger walked into the Barbershop. He gave fives and bounced fist as he walked to the back. Benny sat there behind his desk playing with his computer as usual.

"Danger Que Paso Mi Hermano."

"What's up Benny?"

Right away Benny knew it was more than a social visit, Danger sat down and began to explain everything to Benny from beginning to end, and it was Benny that helped put the plan together. He himself also wanted to get a little revenge it was the Carposi family that murdered his brother and although they did business Benny had been waiting for the opportunity to get back at Junior


"Maybe it was Sandra?", Stagalini said to William.

"No she really knew nothing, sometimes it amazes me how ignorant she truly is", William answered.

"Ahem, maybe she's not as ignorant as you think", Josephine added.

"Someone is leaking info and he or she has to be close to

you",

Stags said as they all contemplated on how Bakemen knew Williams every move.

"Wait we know all the info he had was shit that went on in the office maybe he has your office bugged", Adrian said,

Stags nodding in agreement.

"Men are so ignorant the office bugged oh my God." Josephine said rolling her eyes

"So what do you think it is Josephine?", William added.

"Do you have a secretary?" William nodded.

"Did you hire her or did Bakemen?"

"Bakemen", William answered.

"So now we know how", Josephine said smiling.

After almost three hours, Danger walked into the house carrying a knapsack filled with guns they armed everyone, as Danger explained the plan.

"What's the lighter fluid for?", Adrian asked.

"This is for you William", Danger handed him the lighter fluid and stick lighter.

"What are we having BBQ?", William asked.

"No you'll see."

The plan was set William and Stagalini went to Long Island, Danger and Adrian sat in front of McDonald's on 140th and seventh Ave still unable to find S.T, Danger called Benny as William called his office.

"Mr. Bradshaw everyone is looking for you."

"Listen Lisa just take all my calls today, right now I'm meeting with Stagalini at McDonalds on seventh Ave, oh my God even you're gonna get a promotion after this one",

He gave her a few more details and hung up. It was just a waiting game now fifteen minutes later. Josephine sat outside the Adam Clayton Powell State Building.

"Daniel."

"Yes Ma", he now called Josephine.

"He just walked out with two others and got into his car."

"Thank you Ma"

"Alright baby you guys be safe."

"I will."

Danger called William to tell him everything was going as planned, William and Stags set up. In minutes the continental pulled up the two well-dressed men walked into McDonalds. Adrian and Danger quickly moved, guns drawn Danger jumped into the back seat.

"What the hell is this?", Bakemen asked.

"Shut the fuck up", Danger said jamming the gun into Bakemen's side.

"do you know I am a United States Senator."

"Fuck around you'll be a dead man if you don't shut the fuck up",

Adrian said as he jumped into the driver's seat pulling off and headed to Long Island. Danger used Bakemen's phone to call Benny to let him know the package had been picked up. The next call was to Junior Carposi.

"Yeah this is Junior"

"Hey, you fuckin prick", Danger said friendly.

"Who the fuck is this?"

"It's me, you fuckin cunt", Junior laughed.

"Stop playin, who's this?."

"Ya worst fuckin nightmare a nigga with a motherfuckin gun."

"What the fuck I hope you got what I want."

"I got more than what you want you piece of shit, meet me at your warehouse I'll be there in an hour", Danger hung up.

"Here call Carlos", Danger said passing the phone to Bakemen.

They were almost there, Danger knew Carposi would try to beat them there but it didn't matter William and Stags were there waiting. 35 minutes later Carposi walked into the warehouse alone. "Junior welcome", William said.

"What the fuck is this?", Junior asked,

William and Stags sat in the middle of over 2000 kilos of cocaine all doused with lighter fluid. "This is my going out party", Stags answered.

"Oh yeah you're going out alright", Carposi added.

"So where's the girl", William asked. Junior smiled.

"Is this supposed to be a threat, I mean lighter fluid the lighter am I suppose jump up and give you whatever you want?"

"Listen just bring out Jessica."

Once again Junior smiled.

"Oh you think this is a joke motherfucker?"

(Click, click)

William ignited the lighter and set one of the kilos on fire slamming it on the ground.

Carposi started to flat out laugh now.

"It's not his coke", Stags now said.

"So you're not as stupid as you look", Carposi said.

Just then the rear door opened and in walked Benny with one of his guns holding a pistol to Bobby Rich's head.

"Oh great Benny fuckin Yayo and Bobby fuckin snitch what is this a hustler's fuckin convention just give me Stagalini you'll get the running backs girl and we can all go home."

"Nah not yet were waiting for a few more guest, now go get Jessica and we'll all sit and wait", William said as Stag held his gun aimed on Carposi.

"Alright you want the running backs girl, I got something special just for you."

Junior pulled out his cellular phone and dialed a number.

"Yeah come on in", Carposi said then hung up.

He pushed a button on a remote he pulled out his pocket. The shutter gates slowly began to open an old Econo van with dark tints pulled in. The doors opened first Cheeks stepped out slowly with something duct tape to his hand. As he stepped out further it was a shotgun that was attached to someone.

 William saw first it was a woman attached to the other end of the shotgun,  but it didn't seem like the description he had of Jessica. There was a potato sack over her face. Next Ralph 'the Mouth' stepped out exactly the same, hand taped at the wrist to a shotgun with another woman attached.

"What the fuck is this",

Stags asks as Mouth and Cheeks stood in front of them, with the two women heads covered. "This is my insurance. If anything happens to me or my boys, kiss these two pretty women goodbye", Junior said with a smile.

"Who's the other one Carposi", William asked.

"You'll see soon enough, now can we exchange packages or do you want to continue getting high",

Carposi said gesturing to the kilo of coke still burning on the floor. There was a knock on the gate.

"Who the fuck is this now",

Carposi asked as he pressed the button the gate opened Adrian entered followed by Bakemen and Danger.

"Well, Well, Well look who's on the other side of the gun",

Carposi said pointing his gun at Bakemen.

"Yeah well I'm glad you could join us also", Bakemen replied.

"So now that we're all here what's going on William, you know you're going to jail for a long time after this one", Bakemen added.

"Now we're waiting for just one more person…Carlos", William said.

"Let Jessica go", Adrian yelled at Carposi,

Carposi nodded Cheeks and Ralph 'the Mouth' both removed the bags from the women's heads.

"William", Sandra screamed.

Jessica also screamed as Adrian and Carposi began to yell at each other. Now William screamed there was just too much going on at once.

"Shut the fuck up", Danger screamed and everyone was quiet for a moment.

"Wait…wait, Daniel I gotta another surprise for you."

Carposi walked back to the van.

"Man let my girl go", Adrian said pointing the gun at Cheeks.

"Relax", Danger said.

"Yes everyone, chill out", Benny said.

"You, you….. fuckin spick cunt how fuckin dare you, you a fuckin dead man."

"Hey, hey your all dead men", Carposi added as he pulled a naked S.T. out the back of the van. "Guess where I found him running back", Carposi said with a smile.

"As soon as you left home, your woman had the rappers dick in her throat", Ralph 'the Mouth' said laughing.

"Oh God William what's going on", Sandra had tears in her eyes as well as Jessica.

"What? You're lying", Adrian said looking at Jessica, and she just held her head down. "That's not important right now A we came to take care of business", Danger tried to calm his boy.

"Yep running back he was given it to her good."

"Shut the fuck up Carposi", Danger yelled pointing his gun at Carposi now.

"Even heard her call your name Running back", Carposi now said laughing.

"You dirty motherfucker", Adrian said approaching S.T.

"Is it true", Adrian asked but S.T. said nothing.

Adrian now had his gun trained on S.T.

"No A, not now", Danger said.

"Is it true", Adrian yelled.

"I'll put a bullet in your fuckin head right now, is it true", Adrian put the pistol to S.T.'s head. "No", Jessica screamed, Adrian cocked the hammer back.

"No Adrian don't", she now cried.

"What bitch I threw my life away for your bum ass, now you're begging for this niggas life."

"I love him Adrian please."

"Shut the fuck up Jessica, Adrian we'll handle that later."

Danger said.

"You guys act like the whore's the only snake in the room", Bakemen replied.

"Tell him Bobby tell Daniel, how you set up his dad."

"We knew that already", Danger answered.

"Oh yeah, did you know he's the reason you went to jail too?"

"Daniel you spared me you knew everything Donahue and O'Mayer were gonna kill your dad that's why Bakemen had Donahue killed because Bakemen ordered the hit on your dad, he was worried that if Bradshaw got indictments on Donahue and Stagalini they would squeal on him."

Bakemen smiled.

"Alright you got me, but did you know that Bobby killed your mother because she no longer wanted to be his dope fiend prostitute."

"I loved her Bakemen and you know it", Bobby screamed.

Danger knew it was all true but he had already spared Bobby.

"Please William", Sandra cried.

"Get me out of here."

(Bang)

The shot frightened everyone as they turned to see Adrian standing over S.T.'s lifeless body. "No, No, Nooooo", Danger said realizing his plan was going south.

"Fuck that kill that bitch", Carposi ordered Ralph 'the Mouth'.

(Bang) (Bang)

Two separate shots one blowing off Jessica's head. Adrian screamed as Carposi shot at Stagalini,

(Bang) (Bang)

but both shots missed.

"Chill, chill", Danger screamed.

"William give me Stags take your bitch and we all go fucking home", Carposi said.

No one paid attention to the old man standing in the corner smoking his cigar.

"Wait a minute I think I should have some say in this."

"Who the fuck, are you?", asked Carposi.

"Daddy", Sandra cried.

"It's alright baby."

"Jefferson what are you doing here?", William asked.

"Bradshaw you had it made, the little nappy headed nigger

from Harlem. Out of all the men who didn't have a chance, you had to be the one to try and make a difference. Tsk, tsk, tsk." Who the fuck is this?", Danger asked.

"This is my father in-law….it all makes sense now", William answers as once again Bakemen laughed.

"Shut the fuck up Bakemen your as useless as an extra armpit", Jefferson said.

"Daddy what's going on?"

"Sandra, I know what's going on", William said.

"Well someone tell me who the fuck George Jefferson is?", Carposi said.

"You…. Arrogant, lil shit", Jefferson said to Carposi.

"I was here the day your father took control of the New York Mafia. Together we planned the hit on Pasterelli, the hit that made your dad Boss."

(click, click)

William struck the lighter.

"Don't do it William, don't you fucking dare." Jefferson threatened

"Who the fuck, are you?", Carposi asked.

"He's the man who decided it was time for you to become boss Junior", Bakemen added.

William slammed another kilo into the ground, the powder mixing with the lighter fluid William struck the lighter and again the coke quickly went up in flames.

"No", Jefferson screamed.

"I'm gonna take Sandra and my friends and we're gonna walk out of here."

Jefferson shook his head.

"Too much has been said William, I can't let you go, you know that."

"Daddy", Sandra screamed.

"Sandra shut up", William said threatening as he held another kilo to the air.

"Bradshaw don't you do it."

"Alright", William slammed the package of cocaine on the floor.

"William no! I swear don't you".

"You care more about this coke than your own family", Sandra said in tears.

"Who the fuck is this" Carposi asked.    Jefferson pulled out his gun.

"What do you want?", Danger asked.

"He wants everyone in this room dead, we all know too

much is that right Jefferson, even your daughter."

Jefferson just smiled.

"Daniel we can't win, your plan was good but there's nothing we can do. It's over."

"I told you, you couldn't win years ago William", Bakemen added.

"Just let them go Jefferson."

"How valiant of you, No."

William began to douse more of the powder with lighter fluid.

"William", Jefferson said louder.

"Who the fuck is this William?", Adrian asked.

"Shut the fuck up", Jefferson said pointing the gun at Adrian.

"Fuck it Charles we'll all get high in here", William said clicking the lighter.

"Just kill the Bitch and let's go Jefferson that will quiet him."

(Bang)

The shot hit Bakemen dead center of his forehead his body dropped. Jefferson shot Bakemen without a word.

"One down William."

"Put the fucking gun down", Benny Yayo yelled.

"Who the fuck, are you", Jefferson yelled.

(click)

The flame burst to life.

"Alright alright, Carposi cut her loose", Jefferson screamed.

"What? fuck you! Fuck that bitch and fuck you William."

Now Jefferson pointed the gun at Junior

"Cut my daughter loose or you'll be the last fucking Don." His gun aimed at Junior

"Put the fucking gun down." William pled soaking the entire pile with lighter fluid

"Fuck you", Jefferson said pointing his gun at William.

"Don't do it William."

"Cut her loose Carposi", Adrian screamed.

"Fuck you", Junior answered as William ignited 10 more kilos.

"No, cut her loose", Jefferson screamed approaching Junior with the gun aimed.

"Carlos", Benny screamed

, "drop the fucking gun."

"Carlos", Junior repeated.

"Yeah Charles Jefferson is Carlos Mayorga",

William answered everyone was quiet for a moment.

"Cut her loose", Carposi ordered Mouth

He quickly did as he was told. Sandra ran into Williams arms.

"Now put the fire out", Carlos said to William.

"Put it out", he screamed

Just then gun fire erupted as Carposi fired at Stags, Cheeks fired hitting Adrian in the shoulder. William pushed Sandra to the ground.

"Go",

He yelled to her with her out of sight William set the rest of the cocaine on fire as shots flew in all directions. Benny was down on his knee checking Bobby Rich who was down he looked up to see Carposi standing over him.

"Fuck him", Carposi said pointing his gun at Benny.

"I'm a Federal Agent."

Just then the doors of the warehouse blew open as the Feds stormed in. Danger's plan had almost been perfect. He knew everyone was being watched by the Feds only person they needed was Carlos. William knew the warehouse was bugged so that was the perfect meeting place. They didn't expect Sandra and S.T. to get snatched, S.T.'s griminess had ruined everything.

After months of investigation, a trials was ready to begin.

"The State Calls Federal Agent Benito Arroyo."

"State your name and shield number."

"Benito Arroyo Agent 92172." Benny replied

"What can you tell us about your investigation?" The prosecutor asked

"Well Supreme Court Justice I had been undercover for over 10 years, I had been investigating my own brother which led me to the names of a corrupt congressman Harper Bakemen also a corrupt Police Commissioner Joseph Donahue and a name I had heard some many times growing up as a child in the Dominican Republic Carlos Mayorga. As a child I heard tales of Mayorga's murderous rampages at one point during the seventies Mayorga's Cartel went to war with the Government he had been exiled and never heard from. As I made it through the academy my brother chose the other side of the law and I went after him as I said that led me to Bakemen and Donahue which led me to Ray 'Bobby Rich' Roberts."

Benny paused to sip his water.

"At this time the mafia was slowly losing its power they

literally had no control over the cocaine trade which was taking over the drug game due to the explosive wave of crack cocaine and the Mafia wanted in. After the order by Jimmy 'the Snake' Carposi to kill my brother Agent Spence my commanding officer and I decided I would go deep undercover and the best way to start was for me to get close to Ray Roberts. That was when Spence discovered Danger was Ray Roberts top man."

"And Danger is?"

"Excuse me Daniel Warren."

"Please note that Arroyo is pointing to the son of Martin Warren, well what was discovered once you found out about Daniel Warren?"

"Spence decided it would be easier to infiltrate the drug ring by getting to the lowest man on the totem pole."

"Which was Daniel Warren?"

"Ahem, yes", Benny answered.

Until all evidence was produced all men would be charged as co-defendants, Danger could only shake his head.

"After the murder of my brother I went undercover as my brothers second in charge we set up shop in his Barber Shop on 169th and Clay Avenue in the Bronx. I was incarcerated in Fishkill I was transferred for three months to the facility where Daniel was imprisoned where we became friends working for Ray Roberts he knew my brother so, I told him of prices that I knew his boss wouldn't be able to resist upon Daniel's release."

"During the time you were incarcerated with Daniel had he ever mentioned any connections to the Infamous Decons street gang?"

"Yes."

The crowd finally made a low noise as they all whispered among each other at Benny's answer,

"And what did he say about Decons?"

"On several occasions Daniel expressed his disapproval of the gang's actions while he was incarcerated."

"Would you say he gave you any reason to believe he was the leader of Decons?"

"No", once again the crowd mumbled,

"but on several occasions he told me he was tired of being associated with them."

"Alright what did you find out about Commissioner Donahue."

"Every move Donahue made was conducted by James 'the Snake' Carposi and Senator Harper Bakemen I have audio and video to support my findings."

"What can you tell us about Carlos Mayorga."

There was a long pause.

"He ordered the murder Harper Bakemen."

"Do you have anything to tie him to the drug ring?"

"No", Benny answered.

"Thank you Mr. Arroyo."

Benny left the stand they were still no closer to any conviction of Carlos 'Charles Jefferson' Mayorga. With Harper Bakemen dead as well as Donahue no one could connect him to anything. After listening to audio over and over of the night in the warehouse Jefferson's defense team easily proved Jefferson shot Bakemen in defense of his daughter. So he was looking at manslaughter in the second degree. As bad as they wanted Carlos the more the trials went on the more Danger, Adrian and Junior were incriminated. Once Detective Lipsett took the stand it was over for Junior Carposi. Lipsett told how Junior ordered the hits on Donahue and Stagalini's mom. The Feds had the phone taps and audio from Junior's home to support that. Junior Carposi was sentenced natural life.

"The people call Lance Palmer to the stand."

L.P. approached the bench, for some reason Danger's heart began to pound. L.P. was his man but he had a feeling that it was all wrong.

"State your name."

"Lance 'L.P.' Palmer."

"Are you the leader of the Decons."

"No." The crowd mumbled.

"Is the leader in this courtroom?"

"Yes", without hesitation L.P. pointed to Danger.

"Note that Palmer is pointing to Daniel 'Danger' Warren, did Warren order the hit on rapper Bernard Bless?"

"Yes and the murder of King James when he found out we didn't kill Bless."

"Were you promised anything for your testimony?"

"Yes."

"And what was that?"

"I'd be exonerated for all charges filed against me. I did what I did for fear of my life. Adrian Walker and Daniel Warren are cold blooded killers. Adrian killed his own father for stealing drugs."

After his testimony L.P. was extradited back to Oklahoma to finish his 10 year sentence.

Word of L.P. testifying on Danger quickly spread through the hood. The streets were outraged. Rappers made songs in honor of their fallen soldier. Even Budda Bless dropped a song called the Bible which spoke of the rise and fall of the Harlem and Brooklyn protégés. The song was explicated and got deep into detail about their ties to the drug dealing. It even mentioned some cats in Brooklyn being upset that L.P put a cat from Harlem second in command.  After hearing the song Dangers defense team thought it would be detrimental to his case.  So they subpoenaed Budda Bless who felt to testify would be bad for his bad boy image fled the state.  Still the defense team played the tape.

"The Hood couldn't believe what was L.P. thinking/ Decons is made men, Danger from Harlem what the fuck was Lance drinking/, streets released a beast, I'm hit that's what happens when faggots decide to flip/ oh shit D-Most was the Bitch."

The prosecutors decided the tape was fictitious and not admissible without the testimony of Budda Bless.  Meanwhile Bless was in Vegas partying like a rock star his new Manager Minnesota thought it would be a good idea to film his new video on the late night in Nevada desert for the song,

"The Worlds Against Me" during the entire shoot they kept the camera out of focus so it was hard to tell if it was Budda or not.  After the shoot, Budda and his entourage went back to the Casino, Minnesota thought it was a bad idea and it was after several drinks Minnesota proved to be right.  A drunken Budda walked through the Casino starting trouble.

"What a mutha fuckin coincidence",

Budda said as he bumped into D-Most and his crew. Words exchanged and before anyone knew it D-Most and his boys were stomping and kicking Budda all over the lobby the entire incident was caught on film. After being rushed to Cedar Sinai for minor injuries Las Vegas Police came to arrest Budda, on an arrest warrant from New York. The News aired the incident over and over as Budda laid handcuffed to the bed. Feds came out to question him. He explained the fact that he evaded the subpoena because he didn't want to be involved in the case, he also in Danger's defense told how it was D-Most that ordered the hit on him not, Danger.

"In the street bible you made many references to Decon and Harlem what can you tell us about that?"

"If you want to know anything buy the album the entire story is there."

Needless to say other than that Budda said nothing else. Two weeks later D-Most was beaten with a bat outside a Roscoe's Chicken and Waffles.

The Federal prosecutor was getting desperate Carlos Mayorga was slowly slipping through the cracks. Carlos lawyer put in a motion to dismiss. If the Prosecutor couldn't get anything on him they'd have to give him bail or cut him loose.

"The State calls James 'Jimmy the Snake' Carposi to the stand."

Jimmy 'the Snake' looked as if he'd aged 20 years he looked so fragile he had been locked up 9 years and they hadn't been good to him. After Juniors hit on Don Rizzoto

Jimmy had stopped speaking to his son. He saved his life because the other families wanted him dead but out of respect for the Underboss Jimmy 'the Snake' they let it pass out of respect and 10 million dollars to Damone Rizzoto. As Jimmy's small frame sat on the stand Carlos began to shift in his seat. His underarms began to sweat as well as his palms.

"State your name please."

"James Carposi the second", he said in a low voice.

"Please speak into the microphone", the Bailiff said, Jimmy nodded.

"Raise your right hand…Do you promise to tell the truth, the whole truth, and nothing but the truth, so help you God?"

"Yes",

Jimmy said as the sketch artist doodled away and reporters scribbled on their note pads.

"First sir can I ask you have you been promised anything. Money, freedom anything for your testimony here today?", the prosecutor ask Jimmy shook his head then answered,

"No."

"So why are you here today taking the stand against Charles Jefferson?"

"I'm dying and I feel I should make things right before I

enter the gates of Hell",

the crowd erupted as the judge banged his gavel for quiet.

"So what are you here to tell us?"

"Whatever you need to know."

"Who is that man?", the prosecutor asked pointing at Charles Jefferson.

"That's Carlos Mayorga."

"And how do you know that's his name?"

The courtroom was quiet as they waited to hear Jimmy 'the Snake's' answer.

"Because 30 something years ago I was given the order by Don Rizzoto to go pick up Carlos at a bus station in New Mexico. He had been thrown out of his country and had made his way to the states through Mexico. I know because I was the one who brought the fake birth certificates socials and driver's license. I gave Carlos the name Charles Jefferson that's how I know."

The crowd rumbled and cameras flashed. Once again the Judge banged his gavel and asked for order, finally the prosecutor felt sure he had something on Carlos Mayorga.

"So Mr. Carposi what can you tell us about Carlos Mayorga and the New York drug trade?"

"Ahem", before Jimmy began he cleared his throat.

"Well it was the early eighties dope was going out the door and cocaine was coming in strong, I personally wanted a piece of it, it was amazing how the ghetto was going over this new crack cocaine epidemic but it was almost impossible to get the right connections until Carlos. At the time I myself was at war with the Jamaicans taking over the city. Them and the Blacks moved as if they were secret lovers, I got a call from Officer Phillip O'Mayer the then partner of the late Commissioner Joseph Donahue, O'Mayer wanted to make sure District Attorney Harper Bakemen would be elected to Attorney General. Carlos Mayorga needed a way to transport cocaine under the radar and what would be a better way than to have the A.G. on your team." "When you say make sure Bakemen would become Attorney General what do you mean?"

Jimmy 'the Snake' couldn't help but to laugh.

"C'mon 1979 Alan Croucher. C'mon we all know Bakemen lost but Croucher daughter overdosed and he fell out the race then there was Jeremy Caan we took pictures holding his infant baby all engineered by Carlos Mayorga, but it worked in months we controlled the cocaine trade but O'Mayer had to have Harlem. The young blacks were getting so much money right there in such a small area he couldn't help himself. That's when he hooked up with Martin Warren they set him up bad I'll testify all he wanted to do was get out of the drug game and they set him up. They got that man sitting in jail cause he wanted to be free, let him go."

Jimmy continued to tell of hits Carlos ordered through
Bakemen including Donahue, finally they had the
indictments they needed for Carlos Mayorga.  Three weeks
after his testimony Jimmy 'the Snake' Carposi died of
testicular cancer.  Carlos Mayorga was sentenced to natural
life that was a breath of content with the conviction.
Spence had done what they had set out to do almost ten
years ago.  They found and convicted Carlos Mayorga but
in the process they had built other cases.  Now the trial
began for Daniel 'Danger' Warren he faced 25 years for
conspiracy charges, conspiracy to murder for the murders
of Frances 'Frenchy' Walker and King Arnold James.
Conspiracy to distribute cocaine tax evasion and violation
Rico stature.  At least he wasn't facing life was his
optimistic view at it until he saw the state's first witness.

"The state calls Adrian Walker."

Adrian raised his right hand and poured out an Oscar
winning performance.  The New District Attorney made a
deal with Adrian that granted him immunity if he testified
against Danger.  They offered Danger the same deal to
testify against Adrian.  Danger thought about it but he held
himself responsible for everything that happen.  Had he not
brought Adrian into this drug game he'd probably be in
Miami under a million-dollar contract.  That was Danger's
problem, he took responsibility for things he had no control
of.  Danger felt disrespected that they had even offered him
a deal to testify against his boy.

"Death Before Dishonor" is truly how he felt and his exact

words to the D.A.

"Fuck you suck my dick."

After Adrian's testimony there was no doubt in anyone's mind Danger was finished. As Adrian left the bench Danger wiped a tear from his eye and mouthed the words

"I am my brother's keeper."

35 years to life.

After Jimmy 'the Snakes' testimony Josephine paid an appeals lawyer and got Showtime's sentence overturned so after serving 17 years Showtime was free. The father was finally home but the son was gone. A vicious cycle!
Adrian went back to Alexis who worked in a broker's firm in Mid-town to support Adrian and his baby with Jessica. All over Adrian was disrespected on the radio, on TV. And in songs. He was banned from the streets, it was said he began shooting dope and could be found in dope houses all over the Bronx in the mid 90's. A dope spot was raided as neighbors complained of an odor coming from the apartment. As police rushed the place they found Adrian in a corner, needle still in his arm. He had been dead for a week.

D-Most and Budda's war went on for years. One night after

a Roy Jones Junior fight Budda was gunned down in the driver seat of his Benz over 17 shots hit the car and Budda was pronounced dead on the scene. He went on to be one of the highest grossing rappers of all time. D-Most was in and out of jail, he too had a coke problem that plagued him. The last time I heard he was a parking lot attendant in Nevada, William was disbarred and the Feds could find no charges to bring on him but he knew what was going on so, he lost his license to practice law. He and Sandra and her mother packed up with over 10 million and disappeared.

"So grandpa whatever happened to L.P.", little Daniel asked. Just then Granma walked in, "What's goin on in here."

"Oh Granma, wow grandpa was telling me about Daniel 'Danger' Warren, you know I'm named after him."

"Yes baby I know and you should stop filling that boys head with that madness, now Daniel it time for bed."

"Ah Granma just ten more minutes."

"Boy go on upstairs and get ready for bed."

"Please Grandpa", that pissed Grandma off.

"Daniel King Palmer you get your tail upstairs and get ready for bed and that's it."

"Ahhhh",

little Daniel stomped up the stairs wondering whatever happened to L.P. as Grandpa sat there and smiled as he lit his cigar. He loved his stories and he also made sure to always remember his brothers.

Made in the USA
Columbia, SC
23 October 2020